Tarot at Midnight

21 Short Tales

Edited by Carla Girtman

Tarot at Midnight
21 Short Tales

Editor
Carla Girtman

Cover Art and Illustrations
Eric Girtman

Credits

Tarot at Midnight copyright © 2015

Carla Girtman | Wordsmith Services

Published in the United States of America

ISBN-13:978-0692657911

ISBN-10:0692657916

First Printing

Contents

Introduction

Carla Girtman

Under the protected cloak of midnight, the
petitioner strikes the heavy brass knocker on the darkened
oak door three times. The iron hinges creak against the
weight of the door as it swings open.

"Welcome, traveler," the tarot reader invites the
cloaked figure to come and sit at the single pedestal table.
The deck of cards is placed face down on the smooth
wooden surface in a single stack. With one slender gloved
hand, the petitioner carefully divides the deck into three
varying piles. The tarot reader picks up the middle pile and
places the other two on top, offering the deck to be cut one
more time. The traveler taps the deck with one long finger.

"And what is your question?"

An ivy tendril, like a lock of hair, slides from
beneath the hood. The stranger hastily tucks the green
strand back into place and asks in a breathy, perfumed
voice, "Can you show me the way home?"

In the world of Tarot, all is not what it seems; signs
are hidden in the landscapes, visions are buried just below
the conscious mind, and the magic permeates in the
everywhere. Begin the journey with The Magician in a
swamp filled with music and mystery. Meet the High

Priestess on the small plantation where blood must be sacrificed. Escape to The Empress's flower garden. Wind your way to the medieval faire to find the Hermit and see how the Lovers meet. Let the Chariot guide you to a new destination. Find comfort in Temperance, and catch a plane with Death. Discover that immortality is not wonderful at the Tower. Join the Emperor's fight against world domination and find out just what in The World is in that bucket of chicken.

Meet the fey and the different. Time travel from past to future. Feel the mystical power of Tarot.

The Magician

The Magician is resourceful, decisive, and powerful. This card is emblematic of new beginnings and awareness. But the darker side of this card reveals trickery and deception. Winner of Women on Writing's short story contest, this story reveals magicians on both sides of this card.

Swamp Music
Carla Girtman

Evening was our favorite porch sitting time. Mama rocking in her chair, the same chair that rocked the croup out of me when I was little. The same chair when we cried our eyes out after we found out Daddy had gone to meet his Maker. The same chair when Mama told me she was going to be with Daddy sometime soon.

Twilight was the time when the fog would spin out smoky tendrils like spider silk weaving a gossamer blanket covering our vegetable garden of peas, carrots and cucumbers. Thready ropes of smoke curling about the trees and creeping around the stocky stilts of our house, yet not ever coming onto the porch. Once when I was little, maybe five or six, the fog was sliding in the yard where I was playing. Mama shouted "Honey May!" and scooped me up just as a tendril of smoke had curled around my ankle.

"It's just a little fog, Mama," I said and squirmed my way out of her arms. "See? I'm fine." But I wasn't. That foggy strand said it wanted me back.

"That there's swamp breath," she warned. "and swamp breath will eat you alive." Then she stared out at that gossamer blanket and I seen something behind her eyes that gave me shivers. But I never asked what it was that frightened her 'cause I already knew.

That was ten years ago.

We sat on the porch, Mama in her rocking chair and me on the top step, shelling green peas for tomorrow's supper. The lazy hum of honeybees wending their way home harmonized with the cicadas. Rain frogs joined in the orchestra with mosquitos' drone and dragonflies' fluttering wings. I opened my mind following the swamp melody and added my own harmony. I never told Mama about that swamp music, but I always took advantage of it. In my mind's eye I followed the bee to its home, saw where cicadas lived, and found the fattest frogs. But there was something else out there, deep in the swamp. I felt its magic curl around mine like that fog strand around my ankle all those years ago. A tenor voice unlike one I had ever heard blended with my soprano. Together we harmonized leading all the critters like an orchestra conductor. Then as twilight blend passed into night, so our song dissolved into the growing velvet of night.

Mama sat real still in her chair, her bowl was full of peas; the empty peapods were piled on the ground. "You got the voice of an angel, Honey May," she said, her voice all raspy and breathless from the sickness.

"I'd give it up just to have you well, Mama," I said, twining my hand around hers. Spidery blue veins mapped their way beneath translucent skin which felt like fragile paper. I hiccupped back tears.

"Now, Honey." She patted my hand and coughed from the effort. "Everyone's got to meet their Maker some time. Why don't you make us some tea?"

"I wish—"

"Honey May."

"Yes, Mama. Right away."

Mama always said wishin' don't make it so, but I knew better. Mama knew that too. There's some powerful magic out here in swamp country and Mama had done her share of wishing. Her being barren and all. I know she done went to the swamp and did some powerful wishing. That's how she got me.

But the piper always gets paid. I don't know what she paid for me, but I have an inklin'. Scared Daddy into the swamp and turning up dead. At least that's what Mama said. Sometimes I wondered if he was the price, but with Mama being so sick I was beginning to think he must have been a down payment.

I carried two teacups and the teapot with the cracked lid that had been in the family for generations. I scooped Mama's special tea into her favorite cup, added hot water, and swirled the tea leaves around.

We sat on the back porch sipping our tea listening to the music of the swamp. I let my voice and mind wander on that sultry breeze wishing somehow I could help Mama.

Honey May.

"You say something, Mama?" I asked, rousing from my inner journey.

"No, child," she said, setting her teacup down.

Well, something had called my name. A bone chill settled on my spine just thinking who – or what –it was. I picked the cup up real casual like I was going back to the kitchen.

"Don't you be reading those tea leaves now."

"They say you're going to be just fine."

"Liar," she said with a little laugh that sent her into a coughing spasm.

Those leaves really said her time was coming and coming soon. Not only that, there was a big change coming for me. All that in Mama's cup.

I took the pot and cups into the kitchen. I rinsed the cups out being real careful not to look my tea leaves. Wasn't sure I wanted to know anything else.

I turned toward the door and heard a wind rushing up rattling the shutters. There was a thump and then Mama shouting. "You can't have her!"

"Mama!" I ran out on the porch. The wind whipped stinging tears to my eyes. I squinted and saw Mama's rocking chair toppled over. I looked up above the tree line and there she was, slow spinning in a foggy whirlwind.

I stepped into the yard. Power surged up me like water rising during a flash flood. Don't know what got into me, but I started singing. I sang louder, higher, until it matched the pitch of the wind. Sang like my life depended on it. Like Mama's life depended on it. I sang 'til I thought my voice would give out, but I kept the notes true.

I slipped into my mind's quiet place and I heard the voice from the swamp asking me to come back. "No," I said, "not until Mama is well and stays safe."

Until first song. The voice gave me the shivers.

Mama came twirling down like the ballerina on my music box. She hugged me real tight as I helped her into the house.

We don't talk much about that evening. Mama got better, even looked younger. Every once in a while, she looks out at the swamp like she's listening and then hugs me tight like she'd never let go. I never sing anymore.

But on those evenings when the breeze gets sultry and the critters sing sweet harmony, it's all I can do to not join in. 'Cause that's exactly what the swamp wants.

The High Priestess is wise, intuitive and mysterious. But she has a dark side full of secrets and insecurity. Knowing how to defeat the enemy is important not only on this plane of life, but also on the other side.

Power in the Blood

Genevieve Worthington

"Martha," Mary whimpered. "I hears dogs."

"They's far away," I said, peering over the cold stone well checking to see if the moon's face was in the water. My cotton dress did nothing to protect me against the October chill, but it was the perfect night for mirror seein': all Hallow's Eve right around midnight with the full moon completely visible in the old stone well. Holding the mirror in my left hand, I stuck my finger with a bramble thorn. Blood always made magic more powerful, and I needed to know what would happen to me if I left this ol' rundown plantation for good. Mirror-seein' was the only way to find out.

Mary was whimpering about hearin' the dogs again. I knew she was scared, but she was the only one I could trust to be a lookout for me.

"Hush up," I hissed. I smeared a drop of blood on the back of the mirror and leaned backward, angling the mirror to catch the moon's reflection. Finally, the mirror clouded over with little gray twisters looking like those wicked tornadoes we got here ever so often.

Mama's wrath would be bad enough if she knew I was here practicing mirror seein'. She'd probably just smack my butt and say no one but God needs to know the future. But if Mistress Jackson found out, she would string me up at dawn by my heels and personally whip the devil out of me. Never Master Jackson. Didn't even watch. Rumor had it he was too soft-hearted and left all the disciplining to the Mistress. Said it was part of her household duties.

Every one of us had felt the touch of that whip at one time or another. Didn't matter if they was innocent or not. Not that I want to think evil of her, but I saw a gleam in her eye every time she flicked the whip over someone's flesh. "It is the will of the Lord," she said, "that you should suffer pain on earth to know the joys of heaven." I think she just said that as an excuse to beat us. Here lately she had taken up using a white cloth to wipe ever so gentle over the bleeding flesh and then tuck it in her pocket. I knew what she was doing, and it shook me something fierce. Blood magic.

Magic runs in my family, not that Mama ever used it since she took up Master Jackson's religion. Meemaw, Mama's mama, taught me all the magic she knew of. She warned about using blood magic. "Blood magic can go bad wrong real fast if'n you're not careful," Meemaw always said. I only hoped Mistress knew what she was doing.

"Martha," Mary whined again pulling me out of my thoughts breakin' my seeing link with the mirror. The gray funnel clouds swirled away and left nothing but the full face of the moon laughin' at me.

"I cain't do this if'n you ain't quiet," I said, not moving from my position. "You got them buckets?"

"Yes," Mary whimpered.

"They full?"

"Not yet."

"Then just stan' there and look like you is going to fill ;em. We are just here getting water for the mistress."

"We's just here getting water for Mistress," Mary said the words over and over. I let her repeating words lull me back into the seeing way.

The mirror clouded over with the twisters, and the pictures came. A chill settled in my stomach and my arms prickled, but not from the night wind. There in the mirror I saw Master sitting on a bony looking white horse, but his hands was tied back and he had bare feet. Colors of black and yellow slithered and wormed their way through the picture of this future. This was not a good sign. Mistress was there too, usin' a white cloth to wipe the blood from his leg. She turned, looked right at me, and smiled. "I'm waiting for you," she said, crooking one skinny finger beckoning me to come.

I flung that mirror in the well, my heart pounding in my ears.

"You done?" Mary asked. Her eyes was big and she clutched that water bucket like it might escape. We heard the whine of a dog closer than we cared for and she held that bucket even tighter. "Martha, I'm so skeered."

"I know." I patted her hand. I didn't want her know how scared I was too.

Down the path I saw several men with a pack of hunting dogs coming toward us. "They's just looking for our men folk who went to join up with Union Army."

"How do you know they ain't looking for us?"

I seen the men folk leave," I said, keeping my voice low. "Two nights ago. My baby brother was with 'em." I flung the bucket down the well and hauled water up. "They's not looking for us." I tugged on her bucket. "They's not going to notice us if we's workin'." Mary's hands trembled as I filled her bucket, then mine.

We staggered down the path lugging them buckets as the men and their dogs came up on us. Mary and I stumbled into the brush, thorns snagging at our already raggedy dresses, to get out of their way. One of the hounds snuffled at Martha; I thought she was going to draw blood she bit her lip so hard. I shifted my weight to keep a thorn from digging deeper into my foot. Water slopped onto my dress making me colder than I already was. The dog's owner jerked on the leash pulling it away from Mary.

I whispered one of Meemaw's misleadin' spells causing a rotten branch to fall. One of hounds bayed and strained toward the sound heading away from the stony path. "Looks like they went that way," one of the men said giving his dog some lead. "Let's go."

"They didn't see us," Mary said with a sigh of relief.

"They never see us less'n they want something," I said. "Let's get this water back to the house."

Water sloshed from our buckets as we scampered down the pathway. The buckets might have been half full when we dumped them in the water barrel, but at least it would be one less trip we would have to make in the morning. Mary ran home before I could say thank you and good night. A sliver of light fell on me when Mistress Jackson opened the kitchen door.

"Martha," she said. Her eyes pinched together all hard and mean-looking. "What are you doing up so late?"

"Just getting' a head start on the morning water, Mistress Jackson," I said with a quick curtsey and stared at the ground not meeting her eyes. My heel throbbed where the thorn jabbed it.

"Well, I'm glad you are up. Master Jackson has taken ill. I need you to take care of him."

"Yes, ma'm," I said.

As I stepped into the house, some blood from my foot fell onto the threshold. I grabbed one of the washing rags from the porch rail, scooped up some water with the drinking cup and poured it on the rag.

"What are you doing? I need you now," Mistress Jackson said.

I scrubbed the bloodstain away. Mistress did enough trampling on my life. Didn't need to give her any more power than she already had. "Is bad luck for blood bein' on the threshold, Mistress," I explained as I ripped a piece of my dress and bound up my heel. Didn't want to take any chances of blood falling where it ought not again.

"Nonsense," she huffed, snatching the rag from my hand and throwing it in the kitchen fireplace.

Might have been my imagination, but the rag flared up like a piece of paper. The cinder settled in the grate starin' at me like a glowin' red eye.

"You know how I feel about superstitions. Get upstairs and tend Master Jackson."

I trudged up the stairs thinking back on my vision. Him being sick sure fit in with what I saw. I saw him laying there all pale and wheezing. A mean thought crept into my mind about Mistress doing him in, but that isn't what bothered me so much. It was all the ghosts standing 'round him. I was surprised to see even Meemaw there. She shushed me with one plump finger to her lips and shook her head.

"Cover the mirror," she said, "Don't forget the power of the blood, chil'," and she walked off into nothing.

Seeing ghosts was nothing new; I seen 'em all the time. But carryin' on a conversation with 'em? That would've opened up a whole 'nother door I didn't want to go through.

Dragging out sheets from the closet, I carried them to the water barrel to soak. I spent all night toting heavy, wet sheets one at a time up and down stairs to cool Master Jackson's fever. Mistress had already sent for the doctor, but it would be well into the morning before he'd got here. I wasn't so sure Master would see the sunrise, not the way the ghosts kept poppin' in and out to check on him. I tried everything, even the fever cure spells that Meemaw taught me from the old ways.

I sat on the floor at the end of Master Jackson's bed, tiredness laying over me like the last cold wet sheet I put on the master. Even my foot was too tired to hurt. Then the tall dressing mirror in his room that stood near the door smoked over, dark and black. My bones shuddered and I flung a damp sheet over the mirror. I didn't want to see what I already knew.

Then I saw Mistress Jackson leaning over him calling his name, soft at first, then screaming it. She collapsed on to his body in a weepin' heap. At least it sounded like weepin'. But then I heard a low keen of laughter pour out from her throat.

"You stupid man. Did you think for one minute I would continue playing the role of obedient wife while you frittered away all my daddy's money fighting some stupid war?" She pulled a knife from her pocket. "You wouldn't listen. We could have had everything." She sliced his wrist. "Now *you* will listen. You will be the obedient one." His dead blood welled and dripped into a wooden bowl she held. "And I will have back what belongs to me." She went silent and I glanced up. She was staring at the dressing mirror I had draped with the sheet.

"Martha," she said her voice like cold steel. "Why is the sheet on the mirror?"

"To keep Master Jackson's soul from getting trapped 'tween this world and the next. So he can move on to his reward," I squeaked, pushing against the footboard sliding up to stand.

"His soul is already in heaven." The blood in the bowl quaked in her grip. "Take it off. Now."

I never beg, especially to Mistress Jackson, but this time I did. Master Jackson did not deserve to be trapped in the nether world defenseless against whatever she had planned. No one did. "Please, Mistress, just one day. Just till sunset."

"Take it off," she said. Cold power spilled off her and washed me in icy waves. She buzzed around my thoughts like a hive of bees.

"Power in the blood," Meemaw whispered in my ear and pointed to Mistress' hand. She had a dripping cut smearing her blood on the wooden bowl. I moved faster than I ever thought I could. I grabbed the wet sheet from the mirror and flung it at Mistress Jackson. She dropped the bowl of blood with a howl. With one hand I caught the falling bowl before it spilled onto the floor. I slid my other hand over her cut hand and slapped my bloody palm on the darkened mirror.

Meemaw fluttered around in my head and I said words I didn't know or understand. All I remember was Master Jackson standing next to me, all young and strong, his ghostly arm resting around my shoulders. We watched Mistress being pulled so far into the mirror she disappeared.

"I never realized she hated me so much," Master Jackson said. There was a note of sadness followed by a sigh. He turned around looking into the mirror leaning in as though listening to someone I couldn't hear. It had clouded over in the gray twister color. He hung his head, shaking it. "I understand. It was my arrogance. I should have listened." He breathed out another sad sigh.

I flung the damp sheet over the mirror, more out of habit than anything. I didn't think I needed to worry about him following after Mistress.

Another portal window opened bringin' light brighter than I had ever seen. Master Jackson stood in the light his face all lit up with a happiness.

MeeMaw poked her head out of the light and held out a hand. "We's waiting, Richard," she said, calling Master by his first name. "Come on. We've got lots to do." Meemaw looked so much younger than I had ever remembered seeing her. And happier. She gave me one of her big ol' smiles. "Honey chil', you gets one chance to see your future."

Master stepped through the portal and I watched them both walk down a grassy path into a place I could only call heaven. Clouds puffy and white spilled over the entrance and cleared. There was a thousand thousand futures all filled with healers and other kinds of workers I didn't know what was. But they all had my blood in 'em.

The Empress

The Empress is a card full of hospitality and mother's protective love. If mama's not happy, no one is happy. And there is nothing like a mother's love for her flower garden.

Flower Children

Carol Clark

"I send a bouquet of flowers hoping that they touch your heart
Well the flowers speak louder than words my dear, tell me what keeps us apart..."
- Ferlin Husky

Harris pulled the red Explorer into the dirt driveway, and sighed at the sight of the house. If loose shingles and chipped paint were the outside, he could only imagine the inside. Willa seemed unfazed, and hurriedly unlatched her seatbelt and hopped out of the SUV.

"Wow, it looks spacious. And honey look, there's room for my gardens here!" She smiled, and motioned widely at all the areas for vegetable and flower gardens. Harris watched her. His thoughts about the disheveled state of the house dissipated with his wife's excitement. He hadn't seen her smile in months. He stepped out of the SUV.

The idea to relocate was his. Exhausted by his wife's emotional state and worn down by six years of unsuccessful baby-making, he had talked Willa into moving. She'd finally given in, agreeing that they needed to escape from fertility doctors and friends basking in the glow of newborns. Out here in the country, they could be mid-fortyish together, family enough for each other. Harris had a feeling this was just the place that Willa could come alive again. At this country house. In simple, quiet Nature.

Willa grabbed her husband's hand and pulled him along, pointing to every area of the house.

"Look, over here, this will be our living room. And here! The kitchen faces out to the backyard! You know I've always dreamed of watching the birds and other animals while I'm making dinner."

Willa turned suddenly to Harris, and hugged him. It felt like the first real hug in years, emanating from love rather than a forced prelude to sex. Harris smelled the sweet lavender-vanilla of her hair and caressed her back. She was still in great shape; her forties had been good to her. He didn't want to let her go. Willa was coming back.

The following months passed quickly. Willa went to work on the gardens, and Harris did his consulting work most days. Other days he made multiple trips to Home Depot for home supplies. They came together at dinnertime to share the day's accomplishments over glasses of Cabernet. Perfunctory sex transformed into hours of passionate lovemaking. Willa was alive and gorgeous. Afterwards while she slept, Harrison would sit alone on the front porch, grateful and fulfilled and transfixed by the night sky. He found new star patterns and tried counting the brilliant lights in the sky. An impossible task, but counting his blessings was easy.

The month of April dumped days of rain over their home and Willa's gardens. Colorful buds began to pop up in every direction. Purple tulips, yellow daffodils, and red and orange pansies seemed to grow by the hour. On the hotter days Willa made sure she watered her flowers both morning and evening.

One afternoon, the two drove to town. They needed supplies for home projects, and Harris also concluded early in the morning that it was a good day to get Willa out of the house. She was starting her monthly cycle again, and part of him wished the whole business would just end. He knew he wasn't alone in this thought. That morning after Willa had been crying in the bathroom and come out with her hands clenched on her abdomen, there was no doubt that the evil had returned once again. He'd hopped out of bed instantly and got dressed, suggesting Home Depot and the Garden department. Harris almost couldn't believe the words as they exited his mouth, but perhaps there was a new plant she hadn't tried yet? In the car Willa kept her hands on her stomach and whispered some things to herself. He didn't try to interpret the sounds created from her pain, he simply let her be in her own world. Eventually there would be closure, a finish to this absurdity that yielded nothing for her – for them.

At the home and garden shop, Willa dragged three large bags of soil to the counter.

"Honey, we just bought soil last week. Do we really need all these?"

"Harris, our flowers have to eat, don't they? She sighed loudly and rolled her eyes at him.

He waited to hand the clerk his credit card, shaking his head and ready to commune with someone over his wife's silly behavior. But when the clerk turned to face him, Harris saw her protruding belly. He looked into her face - she couldn't have been more than sixteen. Harris couldn't go back to that business - he wouldn't.

"Uh, honey, I got this. Why don't you start taking bags out to the car, and – "

It was too late. Willa had seen her. She saw every pregnant inch of the young girl's body: large young breasts, and hips perfect for childbearing. The clerk beamed a "hello" to them.

Willa went into action. "Oh, I suppose they let children have children out here?"

Harris grabbed his wife's hand. "Honey, we need to get going..."

"But darling, don't you want to talk to the pretty girl who's going to be a Mommy?"

She's probably got the baby's room fixed up and a name already picked out. Let me see: 'Michael', 'Alicia', or wait, something trendy for you young moms, like 'Connor'? Tell me, do you think…."

Harris nodded an apology to the bewildered clerk. He dragged Willa to the car, leaving the bags of dirt behind.

They were quiet for the ride home. Harris hoped the store was an isolated incident, that when they returned home Willa would shake this off and relax again. She broke the silence that had frozen them both.

"Thanks honey, now we have no food for them. Our flowers can't live on water alone, you know. God." She sighed in disgust, and Harris remained quiet.

* * *

He was awakened at 7AM by bright sunshine that flowed in through their bedroom curtains. She'd already pulled the shades? Harris groaned. I suppose everyone's got to be up with the sun and the flowers. He trudged downstairs to find her dressed in her grey sweatshirt and gardening gloves. She was filling an oversized watering can.

"Good morning, love." She pecked him on the cheek, then went outside.

As he sipped his first cup of coffee, Harris watched his wife from the window. His mood lightened as he saw her hard at work in the soil. This was truly her element. He tried to count the rows of flowers she'd planted, but couldn't. It seemed she used every patch of soil available to cultivate her hobby. He smiled. "That's my girl."

But as the garden patches grew and Willa's days were consumed by flowers and fertilizer, it was inevitable that the thoughts about her "possible obsessiveness" and other suggestions from some of the doctors back in Chicago crept back to his mind. One specialist told Harris his wife was "traumatized" by their infertility, and that neuroses were starting to set in. That scared him the most. They had switched from fertility doctors to psychiatrists. His heart sank as his mind returned to Chicago, back to the noisy streets and weekly visits to Dr. Stein. Back to the dark city filled with ugly problems.

He'd been so lost in thought that he didn't see or hear Willa. She'd popped up at the window, and was "tap-tapping" to get his attention. She laughed a silent laugh through the closed pane. Harris smiled and she blew him a kiss. She looked so happy. Maybe they were set now, maybe Willa was really OK. He left for work, and thought it odd to hear Willie Nelson's "Happiness Lives Next Door" on the radio. Harris hummed along, knowing that happiness must soon be headed to their home as well. It had to.

About two weeks later they were deep into July. It was hot and humid, and Willa was already at work in the gardens. Harris made breakfast and looked out the window at the familiar scene. Willa was bent over, digging and pulling voraciously at weeds. He knocked on the window. He knocked again, harder. But his wife did not come, as she worked hard at the soil. She was like a clockmaker, intricately designing, diagnosing and making things whole again. He imagined all these months with their crop of flowers and new life that Willa might actually pull Hell right out of the earth and make a new heaven for them here. The flowers were gorgeous. Harris never saw so many shades of red, purple and yellow. And in so many shapes and sizes.

He started out the back door to kiss his wife goodbye. Hearing some singing, Harris wondered if she'd brought out the CD player for company. But the closer he got, he realized it was chatter. Maybe a talk show or something.

Once outside, he realized the full intensity of the flowers. Their combined color was so bright in the morning sun he put up an arm to shade his already sun-glassed eyes. Harris walked up behind her, and realized she was chattering too.

"Honey? Willa, are you alright…?

But she didn't turn around. Suddenly the chatter got louder, and it seemed to emanate from every corner of their home. It was here, in the beauty of a simple summer morning, that Harris felt a chill. His body tightened as he listened closer.

"That's it, my lovies. You're OK." Willa patted the soil and began humming a lullaby. Then Harris heard it. The sounds of tiny voices, starting with the tulips on his right, then the pansies to his left. They buzzed out of tune like an undirected chorus.

"Mommy, Mommy, I want snacks. Mommy, I'm tired. Make him stop, he's hitting me!" The chatter turned into screams. Harrison cupped his ears. In horror, he watched as every flower bent towards his wife, a faceless mob except for tiny moving mouths calling out demands. Willa kept at her work, whispering and hushing and filling the needs of her offspring. She was still smiling, and looked up at him.

"Seems like a mother's work is never done."

Harris stumbled inside and struggled to breathe as he dropped his mug on the tile floor. It shattered. Slowly, the emotion of the past seven years rose up from his gut. He started sobbing. The sounds of two hundred crying baby flowers mixed with his wails to create a cacophony that filled the country air. This Nature, their nature, was ruined. Contaminated and consumed by baby flowers. As the hot July sun rose higher in the sky, Harrison collapsed onto the floor, praying for his wife back and also for the season's first frost.

The Emperor

The Emperor card is symbolic of authority and protection as well as achievement. On the flip side, this card can turn authority into tyranny, but from whose prospective?

Kudzu

Seth Nelsen Bingham

The warning siren from the alarm system I had set up around the perimeter of my house jangled me out of my sleep. Again. Stupid eyeball plants. When will they learn I won't give up?

I stumbled down the stairs and flung open the back door, flame thrower ready. Nothing. All I hear is some wind rustling through the trees, what's left of them. The whispers are indistinct, but I've heard it loud enough to know what they're saying. "The war's on, old man."

"I hear you," I yelled lighting my flame thrower for effect. "Just you come on."

I've been fight a war ever since them critter "eyeball plants" showed up on our planet. It was one thing for them to talk to me about how they are going to take over, but it was another to do it. I made it my mission to make sure our planet remained ours. They now have a healthy respect for a flame thrower.

No one knows where they came from. It could be a government project to keep an eye on everyone – just like something the government would do – but the eyeballs are probably from outer space. Anything that creepy must come from outer space.

Of course like any good alien, their only purpose is to take over the world. Everyone knows that. Plants are just more insidious, sneaky about the takeover. Now I know there are people who like green ivy creepy-crawling all over their house and think it looks real nice. Not me. The first time them eyeball plants tried to cover my house, I chopped all of them plants down and set fire to them.

I call the critters "eyeball plants" because that's what they look like. Beautiful, in a creepy kind of way, when you first see them. The leaves are a feathery, deep green vine which climbs walls and fences creating a soft wall of green with hanging globes. Kinda looks like grapes with fringe. Then they "bloom" and there's all these eyeballs watching you. They blink one after another in an almost hypnotic motion with the eyelash fringe waving a breeze. Eyes of all colors that follow you around like sunflowers follow the sun.

Ever since the eyeball plants landed and seeded the countryside, I heard them whisper. Not in my head like you would expect. Thank all that's holy. Then I probably would have to wear a tin foil hat. People think I'm crazy enough as it is. But anyone can hear them if they listen close enough. They whisper things like love and acceptance. You would think it was the hippie sixties all over again trying to trick us into world peace. Didn't happen then, won't happen now.

Now the whole world (well maybe not the *whole* world) thinks these plants are "pretty." There's even a reality show on the care and feeding of them. And that's their plan – getting people to plant them everywhere. But I know better. The eyeballs are nothing but another form of kudzu. You know about kudzu – one of those fast growing vines the government told farmers it was a good forage crop for cows. That's the government – always looking out for us. Like kudzu, the eyeballs are just another invasive species, just nobody thinks about them that way. I once heard an eyeball say it was a turf war between them and kudzu, and they were going to kick kudzu butt.

I knew flame throwers weren't going to be enough to defeat the eyeballs. Not enough manpower or woman power or whatever is politically correct to say these days. I had to think of something else. It was only by accident that I discovered eyeballs could be killed with pickle brine.

There I was sitting on my porch enjoying some homemade pickles holding onto my flame thrower watching out for the eyeball plants. They were trying to take over my yard yet again, and I was burning them down as fast as I could. Wouldn't you know it, one of the little eyeball critters tried to escape and fell right into my pickle jar on the porch. First time I ever caught a live one. So I slammed the jar lid shut just to see what would happen.

Before I could even think about what to do with it, the critter bounced against the lid trying to escape. But after a minute or two, it swam in circles bumping around like it was drunk, its long feathery eyelashes fluttering before it sank to the bottom of the jar. I watched the eyeball haze over and turn red, all snug like inside its green cocoon. Looked like an exotic stuffed olive. I thought to myself, why they look good enough to eat. So I did. The eyeball skin snapped like a crisp grape, had the texture of a black olive with juice, and that perfect salt dill tang. Tasted pretty good. Even gave me a buzz like downing one of those energy drinks. Well, I got this here idea. Instead of trying to incinerate the critters, I invited them to come on in, that I surrendered. Well, I would have thought they were smarter than that to fall for that. But they did.

I caught more critters and tossed them in pickle brine. The younger ones were the easiest to catch and had a sweeter taste and softer texture, but the oldest ones tasted best with the firmer texture. I opened a website, and sold them as exotic olives for ten bucks a jar. By the time the critters caught on to what I was doing, I had got the world hooked on the taste for pickled eyeballs and gave away a free recipe book with every jar. Gotta love the Internet.

I now keep vigilance over my property in my new armored flame throwing tank. Every once in a while, I see eyeballs peeking over the fence. All I got to do is point my flame thrower and they vanish. I still hear them whisper. How they hate my guts. How they want to take me out. But I've started my own whisper campaign about the pickled eyeball wonder cure. Now it's only a matter of time before we take back what's ours. One pickle jar at a time.

The Hierophant is symbolic of a wise counselor who understands how things are done and uses this knowledge to make good choices. However, it is important to be wary of what that advice is and who is giving it.

Sirens

Aaron L. Garrison

The sirens mournful wail outside my window pulled me like an addict's need for a fix. I snapped open the Venetian blinds and watched two black and whites thread their way toward the harbor at the end of town. The police cars' red lights pulsed down the street like heartbeats in need of a jumpstart. I tapped a cigarette from its pack and rolled it between my thumb and forefinger before putting it between my lips. I wanted to light it in the worst way, but thought better of it. I yanked the cord and the blinds clattered back into place. I sat down in the beat-up leather chair I found at Goodwill last week thinking about the case of the missing brains. It wasn't like these guys were stupid. Every single one had a hole punched in his skull and brains slurped out like some kind of ice cream soda.

Smoking helped me think and I needed to think. My secretary, Jenna, couldn't stand cigarette smoke so I had to take it outside. She wasn't the best looker in town, but she could set fire to a keyboard and her voice of honey could just about talk anybody out of anything. And she worked for cheap.

"Going for a walk, Jenna," I growled passing by her desk. "See you in the a.m."

"Night, Mr. Hughes," she chirped as she tidied her desk, a sign she was getting ready to leave. "Be careful out there. I heard there was some weird things going on down at the boardwalk, but no one's talking except clams."

That's Jenna. The one person I could depend on for reliable information. Since I hired her, I was able to earn enough to pay her and the rent. But this case was different. The only clues we had were the victims were men from all walks of life. Rich, poor, in-between. No signs of struggle. No gunshot wounds. Nothing that would have killed them outright except a strange hole in their skull and missing their brains.

The glass office door with the neatly printed "Grant Hughes, Private Detective" rattled closed behind me. I lit my cigarette, breathed in some sweet smoke, and strode down the sidewalk. The sun was moving west and the ocean breeze smacked of salt.

Heading on foot toward the boardwalk, mostly because I had no wheels, I was thinking about the case. The coppers had put up the kind of reward that would tempt anyone to turn in their own mother. My kind of money. I reached the pier with the sun still above the horizon giving me enough light to study the boards and rails to see what the cops missed. They were always missing something. I pulled a drag from my cigarette and continued walking to the end of the boardwalk. Nothing.

I leaned against the wooden rail, sturdy despite the aged wood full of splinters, and squinted against the bright sunset. Just beyond the beach front was a jut of rocks shadowed against the sun which was setting slow, like molasses on a pancake. The ocean waves slapped and crashed against the rocks.

Something moved.

I stared a minute or two at the rocks, but didn't see nothing else move. I shrugged. Must have been a trick with the light. Taking the last drag off my cigarette, I flicked the butt over the rail's edge and watched the tiny red dot tumble into the dark water. Then I saw it. A body riding in on the surf swirling its way under the boardwalk. I phoned the heat with the details and picked my way down to the water's edge.

While I waited for the cops, I heard the sweetest singing a guy ever laid ears on. Visions of all the women I had known – those I had loved, and those I hadn't – swirled inside my head. Made me dizzy. A muffled siren whined, getting closer. Then her voice stopped. I shook myself awake finding myself standing in the water, dumb as a rock.

"What the hell?" Crap. These were my new shoes and I couldn't get any newer ones until next paycheck – whenever that was going to be. What was I thinking? Apparently I wasn't.

I sloshed my way back to the shore, trying to shake the water out of my shoes and trying to remember just why I was there. Someone called my name. Oh yeah, the case. I shook loose of the stupor and faced Mike Austin, chief of police.

"Over here, Chief," I pointed to the latest victim.

"Shiz," Austin said. He looked like he had been punched in the gut. He radioed for the morgue and forensics.

"What? You know who it is?"

"Yeah. It's Brian Sully. He's the patrol officer assigned to this beat."

I gave my statement to one of the cops while someone yellow-taped the crime scene. I knew forensics wouldn't find much. All that was left of poor Sully was a face full of fish nibbles and no brains. I saw the puncture on the top of his head before someone threw a sheet over him.

"You need anything more, Mike?" I asked.

"Naw. Just let me know if you find anything. *Anything*," he emphasized.

Austin and me go way back. We both wanted to solve crimes; he just wanted to be above board. Me, I poked around a lot of times where I shouldn't.

"You know I will," I said. "Sorry about Sully."

I headed toward the beach front. The sun was just a few rays away from being dark. I heard her singing again. I crammed my fat fingers in my ears, but her voice snaked in through the cracks. I was getting that dizzy feeling again when I remembered something from my high school lit class about the Greek fella Odysseus and how he kept his shipmates from hearing the Siren's song. I snapped off a couple of cigarette filters and stuffed them in my ears. Looks like filters could do more than keep out tar and nicotine. Mostly. At least I could think clear.

She sat on largest rock with every luscious curve a man could want silhouetted against the rosy sunset. Even through the filters, I could hear her begging me to come closer. And I did. I remembered all the women I done wrong. Promised to call and didn't. Times I took the rich ones for a couple of grand. I needed their forgiveness, and I needed hers too. I staggered into the water splashing towards her.

As beautiful as she was, there was another curve I didn't expect – a fish tail. Holy crap. A mermaid. My cigarette filters wiggled out of my ears and her song exploded in my skull. But as I reached the rock where she sat, I saw her face and screamed wishing I could claw my eyes out. One eyeball hung by a sinewy thread. Her bones poked through her ribcage and chunks of fish scales slid into the water. I gagged on the putrid smell of decay that overpowered the salt air. I back peddled, but she grabbed my arm and pulled me next to her with a strength women shouldn't have.

"Hello, lover," her voice rasped like she had sung for too many whiskeys in a smoky bar. Pulling me closer; her tongue slobbered around my neck and up my face. "You're real tasty." She gave me a seductive smile before her bottom lip quivered and fell into the ocean.

Her front tooth popped out, sharp like a pointed straw, but at least she wasn't singing. Shaking the fuzz from my brain, I reached around her in a weird lover's embrace, cupped my hands around her head, and ran my fingers through the wet strands of her pale green hair. With a sharp twist, her head snapped off with a wet popping sound. I held her head up by the hair like some kind of Greek hero holding Medusa's head. The rest of her body crumpled on the rock like a rotted fish. I called the chief.

"Hughes, you sound like you've had too much to drink," Austin said. "Go home and sleep it off." He hung up.

I fumbled in my pocket for my camera. Crap. Left it at the office. Well, at least I had her head. I staggered back to shore heading to the police station.

"Hughes, honey," Jenna stood on the shore looking – different. All soft and curvy against the rising moonlight.

"Jenna? What are you doing here?" I asked.

She stared at the mermaid's head in my hand. Her laugh, smoky and dark, gave me the shivers. "I see you met my sister," she said in her milk and honey voice. "Good riddance. I warned her about moving in on my territory." She took her sister's head from my hand and chucked it into the water. It spun around a boardwalk piling once before sinking.

"Wait. I need that." Water sloshed up my knees before she stopped me mid-step.

"No you don't," she said and hummed some kind of strange tune.

My legs turned to jelly and dizziness buzzed in my head. I couldn't move.

"Hughes, honey, you did me a big favor killing her like you did," she said. "So I'll make this easy on you."

Her eyes took on a weird sheen. Kinda veiled and shiny all that the same time. I sagged to sit down onto something cold and muscular wrapped around my legs; it was her tail.

"I don't need brains like she did, but I do need something else." Her song spilled over in my head worming its way through my brain.

Jenna caressed my face, her lips soft against my neck. "I did tell you to be careful and I would love to help you out," she said with a throaty hum, tilting my head to the side. Her two front teeth, like little sharp straws, popped out. "But I am so very hungry."

Crap.

The Lovers

The Lovers is all about love, desire, and physical attraction. But patience and the willingness to wait for that one special person will lead to that perfect true love.

Openings
Carla Girtman

There was a doctor who longed for his true love. He had offers and blind dates, but remained alone and lonely.

His last patient was a woman. She sat on the examining table showing signs of cardiac distress.

As he leaned in to listen to her heart, something clinked against his stethoscope. He opened her paper gown, and centered between her breasts was a heart-shaped lock.

She blushed. "Mama always said there was someone who has the key to my heart."

He slipped off his glove, revealing his key-shaped finger. "Papa always said I would unlock my true love's heart."

The Chariot is a card of change and good news for some and delays and frustrations for others. Walk through the Open Door where moving on has a different meaning.

Open Door
Seth Nelsen Bingham

Geoff pounded down the neighborhood hiking trail on his evening run. It wasn't enough that he was forced into mandatory retirement by the police department. He was more competent and in better shape than most of the younger officers who didn't have half the knowledge and experience he had. He was still young, only fifty-five, but no one wanted him. Even though age discrimination was illegal, it didn't take a rocket scientist to figure out that his age was the real reason why no offers were coming his way.

So he hung an investigator shingle out and lived in the upstairs apartment from his office, but building clientele was slow going. He took some classes in business, computers, and investigation to keep his mind from turning to jelly. Money wasn't a problem: no debt and sound investments kept him solvent. He needed action. Some kind of focus. He had only one client in the last six months that lasted three days. He needed action and spying on unfaithful spouses wasn't enough.

Running helped him think and the ground felt good beneath his feet as he followed the dirt trail. He thought about the last interview. Two guys in black suits had come into his office this morning and talked to him. Said they were from Intergalactic Security. Who the heck was Intergalactic Security?

"I'm not interested in being a mall cop," he said. He saw what had happened to other retired police officers who went that route. Got fat and lazy.

"It won't be like that at all," one of them had said. "We like what we've seen of your work, but we need you to pass a test. We will be in touch."

A test. They didn't say what kind of test nor when it was. What did they want him to do, identify little green men?

Sundown was still at least three hours away. Geoff ran listening to the crunch of dry leaves beneath his feet, the cool autumn air against his face.

The path was becoming narrow. Not many ran this far and he would need to turn back. No sooner had he turned around to go home, when he ran into a creature. Rather it ran into him. It sprawled head over heels tumbling toward a rocky ravine. Geoff grabbed the creature by a skinny arm, its oversized coat billowing around an equally skinny frame, before it fell. Its wide brimmed conical hat went flying revealing saucer-shaped eyes that changed in a kaleidoscope of colors. Even as he held its arm, its body constantly shifted shape and size. His cop instincts kicked in as the creature reached into the half-torn pocket of its oversized coat, and he rolled the creature to the ground before it could pull anything out. It was like holding a shifting bag of sand, but he held on. The creature stopped struggling.

"Not to worry, Earther," the creature said. "Only doorknob." It pulled out a sparkling glass multi-faceted doorknob. "See? Can let go me now?"

Geoff wasn't sure. His sixth sense told him this creature, whatever it was, was up to no good. He held onto one shifting arm, hauling it up. "What does it do?"

The creature laughed. "Opens door." It shoved the doorknob into a nearby tree. The glass glowed white hot. Its gnarly fingers twisted the doorknob. Sunlight spilled out of a doorway. The creature peered in. "See, home! Want come? Promise good time." One of its kaleidoscope eyes winked as though sharing a secret. It gave him a goofy twisted smile.

"No, thanks," Geoff said. "Here's fine."

The knob popped into the creature's hand and it tossed the glittery knob at Geoff. As he grabbed it, the creature slipped from his grasp jumping through the entrance. The tree door slammed shut. There was a glittery line that outlined the door shape, but it was fading.

Geoff heard a muffled conversation and pressed his ear against the nearly invisible door.

"Hi, honey! Home!"

"Where been you?"

"Have magic doorknob—"

"Liar!"

Something heavy thumped inside the tree trunk and broke. It sounded like a plate. The tree trunk with its glowing outline vibrated under a fierce pounding from the other side. Geoff stepped back.

"Quick quick! Use knob. Open door!" the creature shouted. "Open only few seconds!"

Geoff jammed the doorknob in and twisted it. The creature fell through. A large vase sailed through the opening. Geoff ducked just in time and the vase smashed into an opposite tree. The tree trunk door closed with a *tthwift*. The doorknob popped into Geoff's hand. But no matter where he put the knob, the tree refused to accept it again.

"No good. Won't work after door closed." The creature sighed and slumped against the tree, its conical hat flopped between its two knobby knees. "Thought she take it better."

"Women," Geoff sympathized.

"Yeah, women. Well, back I take knob now." The creature reached for the doorknob Geoff still held.

"Not so fast." He clamped his hand on the creature's arm to prevent it escaping. "Can you prove you own this?"

The creature squirmed under Geoff's iron grip. "Need to leave now."

The air rippled into a shimmering doorway across from them and two figures stepped through. He recognized them as the two men in suits who visited him earlier. The creature whimpered, shifted, and struggled, but Geoff hung on to him despite his quicksand-like body.

"Congratulations." It was the director of Intergalactic Security. "I'd say you passed with flying colors."

"I don't understand. He's the test?"

"Not exactly. Just the right place at the right time," the director said. "We've been trying to catch him for months." He pointed at the creature and spoke its name in a language that Geoff couldn't understand. "He stole that doorkey last year. We've been able to track him, but were always just seconds behind where he was. Lucky you and he ran into each other."

The assistant picked up a shard of the broken vase and pointed it at the creature. "Wife still won't take you back?"

It sighed and hung its bulbous head. "No, still mad. Going jail?"

" 'fraid so." The director motioned to his assistant who used special restraints on its skinny arms. The two disappeared through the shimmering doorway.

"Good thing you didn't go through his doorway. Without proper training, it could have been years before you found your way back. Maybe never."

Geoff handed the director the glass doorkey knob who pocketed it.

"I like a man who can meet a challenge. Interested in this kind of work?"

Geoff didn't have to be asked twice.

The Strength card can be symbolic of power. But whether that power is used for good or evil, it is in the mind of the beholder – literally.

Roller Coaster

Arron L. Garrison

I got cocky, throwing my weight around and making demands I shouldn't have been making. So my boss just wanted to take me down a peg and assigned me to Earth to give our clients the ultimate primitive experience. Ever since sentient beings were discovered on Earth, everyone, and I mean everyone, wanted an Earther experience. I have nothing against corporal beings, but there is just something about Earthers that just is so – basic.

My job is to transmit emotional experiences, by residing in the source as a psychic connection. I've been in different sentient beings, energy and corporal. Despite my aversion to using Earthers, they were the best experience source: one they don't seem to notice the psychic connection (except for psychics and schizophrenics), two – because their thoughts are so erratic and emotions are this side of primitive, I can deliver a deeper, more satisfying experience to our clients, and three I can disrupt their motor skills like walking. Some of the biggest laughs I get for a client is having an Earther trip over their own feet.

Mind you, I'm good at my job. Very good. And the money's great, but there's more to life than money. My boss has been riding me pretty hard. Right now all I want is a vacation to bask in the glory of my own self. All I had to do was to get through this stint on Earth. Which according to my boss could last about ten years. Might as well be an eternity.

My frontal lobe buzzed. It was J'dk.

"L'rie. Client wants to experience a multi-car crash, no death experience. Minimum five angles."

Let me tell you, neighboring with one Earth mind is like cuddling a spinycat, let alone being in five at one time. "Shades of night! That's intensity plus!"

"Client's a triple pay, bonus if he breaks a sweat."

"I'll need at least two vectors, probably three to recover. Regardless." A five angle would drain me dry for a day or two, but J'dk didn't need to know that. A little vacation with just me and my thoughts and triple pay with a bonus for a couple of Earth months would be perfect.

"No problem. That's why you are the best, L'rie."

"Let me check possibilities."

I remote-viewed traffic from around the world. I located a woman driving a small sports car who was talking on a cell phone. Earthers. If I didn't know better, you would think these creatures always had a glass box attached to their ear. Behind her was a truck driver, on the sidewalk were a couple of customers standing in front of a vegetable and fruit stand. The vendor was helping one of them. Everyone was in easy reach.

I ran some calculations of the odds of an impending accident, angles of attack, and who would be the best anchor. Of course it was the woman on the cell phone. Those people never paid attention to what was going on around them. Perfect. I nestled into her thoughts and anchored myself to her optic nerve, then weaved a connection to the other four and ran a check to make sure I could move smoothly from one Earther to the other. Sliding back into my anchor, I readied her foot to slip from the brake to the accelerator. Earthers had a funny phrase for that action: pedal misapplication. I laughed. This was going to be great. I buzzed J'dk. "All right. Everything's a go. Client ready?"

"Patching through now."

I felt the client's psyche slip into place, his slender electron tendril had a thread of heat spill over as he connected to the experience corridor. His tendril buzzed erratically with anticipation.

"Relax so you can get the full effect," I instructed. "You don't want your own emotion to dampen the experience."

"Right. Sorry." His tendril trembled when he took a proverbial deep breath and cooled ever so slightly.

"Hold on!"

As predicted, the woman was more interested in her cell phone conversation than driving. She glanced up, too late, to see she was too close to the car in front of her. Instead of hitting the brake, she pressed the accelerator. Screaming, she careened around the car ahead of her only to crash into the fruit stand. I tightened my connection and channeled all the emotion from driver to fruit vendor into my client. My client gasped as he felt the vendor's pain explode in his leg as it shattered under the wheel of cell woman's car.

The box truck behind cell phone woman had been following too close and slammed on brakes only to slide toward cell woman's car. I leaped into one of the fruit vendor's customers who had been reaching for a kumquat. The box truck sideswiped him, pressing him into the box of kumquats breaking his arm. My client gasped at the man's pain shot through the experience corridor. Then I bounced into the driver who was directly behind cell phone woman. I helped him gain control to get him away from the kumquat customer only to have him plow into cell woman's car. He wasn't wearing his seatbelt, banged his head against the windshield. A web of cracks splintered where his head hit.

Sirens blared down the street alternating between police, ambulance, and fire truck. I counted the sirens and came up with at least four, but there could have been more. People shouted, screamed, and ran around not knowing what to do. At least a dozen people were on their phones taking video. I was able to tag one of the video takers for five seconds to give the client a view of the cell phone video. As a crowning touch, I caused the driver from the truck stagger out of his car over to cell phone woman's car and sprawled over her hood, blood from his head wound splattering over her windshield.

It was glorious.

The client gasped as the funnel of cacophony of noise, sight, and smell poured over him, nearly drowning him in sensation. His electrons blazed under the sensory overload stimulation.

"Brilliant! Everything and more," the client said. Simply brilliant."

As promised, J'dk sent me to an all-expense paid vacation to my favorite spot where I basked in a pool of quiet. I coalesced into a physical form to enjoy a full body massage. That was one thing the Earthers got right. Nothing in the corporal world even came close to the sensation of someone kneading your flesh.

My front lobe jangled.

"L'rie!" It was J'dk. "Clients are lining up out the door for the Earther experience. I've got you booked through next twenty years."

Shades of night. I'll never get away from Earth.

The Hermit

The Hermit can signify the desire for peace and solitude, but also can serve as a warning against making hasty decisions. The reverse of this card can indicated stubbornness, suspicion, or fear. Can the advice of a magician save Abby from another blind date gone bad?

Cloaked

Lin Neiswender

"Let's meet Saturday- the Renaissance Faire. Wizard's Cave, 7 pm. Looking forward to our first meeting, Beautiful!" Abby stared at the email she'd just printed and tucked it in her bag.

Tomorrow I'll visit that huge costume/vintage clothing shop on the East Side. They should have something that will dazzle him. Hope he's really as handsome as his photo. Sure writes a good game, anyway, she thought to herself. Her fantasies ran wild that night filled with knights in shining armor and a different spin on Cinderella.

Abby rummaged through the antique dresses and old stage costumes, finally settling on a gypsy patchwork skirt and a tight bodice in blue. She stood in front of the full length mirror, but her image didn't feel complete. She wandered into the back of the store where the smell of age, mold, and mothballs filled the room. She opened wooden chests and brittle leather valises with the ambition of a child opening Christmas presents.

Then she found it: an old floor-length cloak, in a deep brown velvet shimmering under the fluorescent light. Abby examined the faded embroidery around the neckline, but all she could make out was the sign for Virgo and something that looked like the Star of David. Faded or not, it was perfect. She didn't even try it on, convinced that this was the right garment. Forty dollars later, it was hers.

Abby splurged on a cab to the Faire, the cloak folded neatly on the seat beside her. The night was going to be warm, and she knew wearing the velvet cloak would make her too hot. She smiled. She hoped she would be hot in a different way when she met Blaise. She paid the cabbie in cash and slipped on the cloak. It seemed lighter and cooler than she thought, and it made her feel odd. She couldn't quite put her finger on why. She pulled her shoulders back to project confidence. Showtime.

Abby flounced her way through the entry gate tossing her ticket in the trash barrel. She couldn't believe they wouldn't take her prepaid ticket at the gate. Then wine wench ignored her in the refreshment tent, and people pushed past her without so much of an "excuse me." It was like she wasn't even there.

She stopped by an antique jewelry display to buy something that would make her feel better and add a final touch to her costume. The seller said nothing to her as she picked up several necklaces that caught her eye. Abby leaned into the mirror to compare the necklaces against her blue bodice, holding back a small scream. She had no reflection.

Oh my god, I'm invisible! She pulled the necklace from her neck. Its image suspended in midair and she still had no reflection. She put the necklace against her throat. It disappeared. What was making her invisible? Then it struck her. It has to be the cloak. Abby pulled it from her shoulders and draped it over her arm.

"Can I help you, Miss?" the shopkeeper asked.

Abby signed with relief and bought the necklace she had in her hand.

I don't understand why or how this is happening, maybe this is a good thing. I think I'll use it to check out Blaise. See if he's all he claims he is. Abby slipped the cloak back on and made her way to the Wizard's Cave. The Cave had five steps leading up to a faux stone platform.

At the bottom of the steps was Blaise, dressed in a ridiculous court jester costume. He paced the landing dragging a little white dog along with him. He kept slipping on the stone platform from the slick soles of his high boots and grabbed the hand rails several times to keep from falling down. His cell phone was clamped to one ear watching anxiously for her arrival. Abby stepped closer to hear his conversation.

"Yeah, the dog is working great. Thanks for the idea. Chicks have been falling all over him and me. I'll get him back to your girlfriend tomorrow. Buy him a big steak if I score! Yeah, later."

Blaise hung up and dialed another number. "Hey baby, it's me." He laughed. "Yeah, got a meeting at the Medieval Faire. It's a laugh alright." He held the camera up and took a selfie. "Yeah, I know. Stupid looking. But it was the only costume they had left. You know how clients are. Yeah, I miss you too. I'll try to ditch this meeting if I can."

Abby stifled back her disappointment. Blaise was exactly what she didn't want him to be. She turned at the sound of a firecracker followed by a puff of smoke.

The Wizard made a grand entrance from the Cave muttering a pseudo-spell. He appeared old, had a long beard, dressed in a monk's hooded robe, and held a long walking stick. Beside him rested a large lantern, casting giant shadows on the walls of the grotto. He stood in the highest point of the cave, quite an imposing figure. Coming down from his perch, the Wizard stood in the doorway, and said, "Come in, come in, your life is to begin, let the Wizard tell you all!" He pointed to Blaise. "You, Blaise. Come in for a reading. Learn your future."

Abby was surprised. How did he know Blaise's name? Then the old man winked at her. Her mouth dropped open. How could he see her? She was still wearing the cloak.

"Shut up, you old bastard, can't you see I'm on the phone!" Blaise growled, slipped, and stepped on the dog's tail. It yelped, pulled free, and ran into the Wizard's Cave. Blaise didn't even notice and continued sweet-talking his backup date.

Blaise's rudeness to the old man shocked her. "You are a jackass!" Abby said, throwing off her cloak.

"Baby, so glad to finally see you," he said with a wide smile, ending his conversation midsentence. "You're even prettier than your picture." He reached out to take her hand, but she pushed him away.

"Take a hike. Don't want to intrude on your real date of the evening," Abby said. "And don't even think about emailing me again."

Blaise shrugged his shoulders, "Your loss," he hissed as he passed her, raising the phone to his ear. "Hey, babe. My client just cancelled on me."

"Young woman, come up here and learn about your future. It is better than you might be expecting!" The Wizard beckoned her in with a flash of light.

Why not? I might as well get something out of this evening. Abby climbed up the steps and stepped into the Cave. She sat in the chair he gestured to and folded the cloak in her lap. The little white dog jumped into her lap and she stroked his soft fur.

"I have to reclaim that cloak, I'm afraid. I've been missing it for years. I'm so glad you have brought it back to me."

Abby couldn't contain her surprise. "How is it yours? I just bought it. It's mine!"

"I can prove it's mine, my dear child," the Wizard said with a tired smile. "Look in the pocket. There is a locket pinned at the bottom."

Abby tuned the pocket inside out and found a very old locket. She undid the pin that secured it to the pocket and the locket fell into her palm. She pried it open with one fingernail. Inside were two portraits: one of the Wizard and one of Blaise in his fool's costume. She looked at him suspicious of his motives. With this cloak, there's no telling what kind of information she could find out now on her dates.

"But how is this possible? You had no way of getting this into my pocket." She frowned and held the cloak tighter. "Are you really a wizard?"

The old man smiled. "I am a just an old man who prefers the solitude of the mountains, but has to keep his son out of trouble. He stole the cloak and pawned it somewhere and it made its way to the vintage store where you bought it. I will gladly repay whatever money you spent. It was about 40 dollars right?" He reached into his pocket and pulled out two crisp twenties, then added another twenty. "Another twenty for your trouble." He held out the money." Please. Now that your eyes have been opened, and you will no longer need the cloak to find your true love. I need the cloak now because I am cold now that my bones have grown so old."

"How did you know that's what I wanted to do with the cloak?" Abby said. Her gut was telling her the old man was telling the truth. She took the money and handed him the cloak.

"Wizards never tell their secrets." He gave her a grandfatherly wink. "Just know you and Blaise were never meant to have a relationship. But you wouldn't have known that if you hadn't had the cloak to hide you to see Blaise in his true personality. Things will work out for you."

The old man pulled out a crystal ball which swirled with smoke. Stroking it, the smoke cleared. The Wizard sighed. "I see Blaise is in trouble again."

"Why don't you just let him deal with the consequences of his actions?" she asked. "Maybe he just needs a kick in the butt instead of you rescuing him."

The Wizard frowned and then brightened. "I see you are wiser than I. Perhaps you are right. He doesn't have any magical abilities, unless you count the gift of gab."

Abby rose to leave. "Are you sure things will work out for me?"

"Quite sure. The cloak has opened your eyes. Trust yourself and that little voice within you."

He put the cloak around him. "Oh yes, now I am warmer."

To her surprise, Abby could still see him in a transparent sort of way.

"Yes, shocking, isn't it? Cloak wearers past and present can always see one another even when only one is wearing the cloak. There is a cloak-wearer out there for you, my dear, never fear. "

He pinned the locket to her bodice. His blue eyes crinkled with delight. She watched his eyes shift color, and felt a tingle shiver through her.

"There, now you have a lucky charm to remember today. I'm sure we will meet again." He embraced Abby and kissed her forehead. "At your wedding."

She fingered the locket pinned against her bodice and she hugged the Wizard good bye. "Thank you," she said.

Stepping out of the Cave, Abby nearly tumbled down the stairs. Someone caught her before she fell.

"You all right, Miss?"

Abby stared into the most magical blue eyes she had ever seen. She shivered watching them shift from a transparent blue to sky blue to ocean blue and back again. His eyes reminded her of the Wizard's. *There is a cloak-wearer out there for you, my dear. Trust your heart.*

She looked up at the Wizard's Cave, but it had disappeared.

"Indeed," she said, accepting his proffered hand. "Can I buy my knight in shining armor a coffee?"

The Wheel of Fortune

Sometimes it is not anything you have done; it just is the way it is – destiny, fate, chance. The Wheel of Fortune card can symbolize a new cycle that can be good or bad depending on how you want look at it.

Losing Count
Carol Clark

"Cheers!"

Robert didn't raise his glass when they toasted on his birthday. After all, it was a cold and dreary November 28, 2001. The crowd of fifty or so guests lifted their glasses not to career advancement or other success, only to the fact that he turned another year older today. He suspected some were here to celebrate that he could actually be here, Robert Hollinger, living and breathing on his fifty-fifth birthday. The truth was he'd been fortunate to have been on a business trip in San Diego when the twin towers collapsed over two months ago. He figured a person didn't get much luckier than that.

But he didn't feel lucky. And he certainly didn't want this party. The soiree was Helen's idea, and he let her go ahead with it.

Robert stood in a funeral-like greeting line, saying hello to some people he barely knew. He watched Helen, and as soon as she disappeared into the oblivion of idle chit-chat with friends, he filled two more champagne glasses and left the room. He wanted to be alone, and knew just the place.

Robert climbed the winding stairs and paused at the top landing. Months ago he would have turned left into the luxury of their spacious bedroom. Now he turned right, into his son Nathan's room. He was greeted by its signature stench, the smell of teenage languor and laziness, plus one dirty hamster called 'Haley.' But Robert didn't mind; in fact, he'd had grown to appreciate the chaos that surrounded him in this room. It comforted him. He stepped through dirty tee-shirts and socks, and after taking a long drink of champagne, sat down on the bed. Closing his eyes, he listened to the celebratory sounds of laughter and music from downstairs. Robert winced. He didn't want to hear any of it, and he certainly didn't want to be happy. With another gulp of champagne, he looked over at Haley's cage.

Haley must have heard him come in because she got up on her hind legs and stared at him for a moment. Robert stared back. *What a stupid little creature, just eating, sleeping, and wasting time on that senseless wheel.* He wondered if the rodent ever thought or felt anything, trapped in her little cage in her little hamster world. Haley hopped up on the wheel and started pedaling. She moved slowly at first, and the wheel creaked in response. But Haley built momentum, and soon the wheel was spinning easier, smoother, until Robert heard its soothing whir. He watched the grey blur move around and around, its effect hypnotic. Though the noise still came from downstairs, Robert had tuned much of it out by now. Five minutes later, with Haley spinning

furiously on her wheel, he relaxed and fell asleep.

* * *

Robert's morning commute by train had changed over the last few months. Since the party, he'd stopped reading his copy of *The Times*, instead laying it down on the seat beside him. He preferred to stare out the train window and think of nothing. Then, around mid-February, along with his outward gaze, there arose a rather sudden and urgent need to count. Numbers popped up in his mind, not random ones, but single digits starting with one.

At first he counted the stations that passed, which added up to ten once he got downtown. But in the past few days the compulsion to count became insistent, almost distressing. Without knowing why, Robert realized he needed to count anything, as long as he reached 88. He tallied buildings and houses as well as the occasional fire truck or ambulance he glimpsed outside the speeding train. Robert's awareness of other commuters and conversations slowly faded, as he gave in to the numbers. Each morning when he reached 88, he could sit back and relax in his seat. He was ready to start another day.

Robert never told Helen or anyone else about the counting. Helen did remark to him about being withdrawn and quiet, and why wasn't he happy these days? She'd suggested therapy (only because her many friends indulged in it), but he just shook his head and smiled. "I'm fine."

On a warm misty morning in April, Robert boarded the 8:05 train as usual. Newspaper in hand, he took his window seat and gazed out the smudged glass. It was overcast and rather dismal outside, but the forecast had promised the clouds would give way to stark sunshine later.

He had trouble believing this, but the weather didn't matter to him much anymore. A day was just another day. He started counting. House by house, building by building, he racked up his numbers. He reached fifty when he heard the screech of the train's brakes, bringing the cars to a halt. The interior lights flickered on and off, until they went out completely. He heard the announcement over the loudspeaker.

"Everyone please remain seated and calm. We're experiencing some minor electrical problems. There will be a slight delay." Groans rose up from every area of the train. While the others moaned and complained, Robert felt a surge of panic. He struggled to suppress his rising anxiety. He'd never gotten stuck in mid-count, always completing the ritual. His breath came faster, and dizziness set in. That was when it dawned on him: he had nothing to count.

Robert felt himself getting hotter. With eyes shut tight and body starting to shake, he tried constructing buildings in his mind. But none took enough shape or form that he could count. His heart beat faster. He tried imagining houses, trees, even telephone poles. But his internal vision had blurred, his mind unable to form clear images. As the expected and mundane moans and complaints continued around him, Robert sank into despair. He couldn't finish counting.

Then it was like someone flipped a switch. Blackness turned to bright white inside Robert's mind and he saw them, heard them all. His friends: Gary, Wanda, Angela, and his boss Jay, screaming and running in different directions. He saw an elevator that was on fire.

"I can't reach you!" Robert shouted, enough to startle and silence the other commuters.

"I'm not there; I want to help you, but I can't reach you! Gary, Jay, Angie!"

The woman in the aisle seat ran to Robert's side.

"Sir, sir, it's alright. Just a power outage. There's no need to panic, you're alright." The woman's words mixed with the white rage in his mind. He struggled to dim the light, to calm the confusion, but he couldn't. The noises of a terror and collapse that he didn't even witness engulfed him. And there it was, the calamity of it all. He'd been miles away from the towers on September 11th. But he could see it all clearly now. With his last bit of energy, he tried to count.

"51, 51..." He collapsed back on the seat, sweating. "51." In the stark white of his mind the numbers accomplished nothing. They lost their power, giving way to the real faces of his friends and colleagues. Some were alive and running for safety. Others were already gone. He reached out to each one of them, alive and dead, touching each hand and saying goodbye. Then the white light that had been so intense faded. He was back on the train, surrounded by strangers who had no faces or figures in the dark.

"I couldn't help them, I couldn't save them. I'm so sorry." Robert sobbed. "No one could reach them on the 88th floor. It was too high. I'm so, so sorry." He continued crying, as strangers around him tried to offer support.

* * *

Robert got home just before eight. He was calmer, had pulled himself together, and made a point to approach Helen tonight. She was reading in the study, and sat up when he walked in. With tear-soaked face, coat on and briefcase in hand, Robert began to speak.

"I'm sorry, hon, sorry I've been so – withdrawn." He paused to catch his breath and stared at the carpet. "But I think I'm OK now."

Helen tossed her book aside, and jumped up to hug him. They clung to each other for a few seconds.

"I love you, Helen." Robert looked into her eyes briefly, then pulled away. "But I *am* tired, it's been a long day." He kissed his wife goodnight, leaving her somewhat stunned but smiling in her chair.

Robert made his way up to the bedroom, and paused at the top of the stairs to hear Haley spinning on her wheel. He went into his son's room. Robert looked at the tiny hamster, crammed in her dirty cage with just a food bowl, some water and the intrepid wheel. Beyond that, she was trapped inside a messy room. Robert choked back tears and spoke to her.

"My dear Haley, I wish I could take you off that wheel and out of this room. You should see everything out there – more critters, lots of grass, and even bright sunshine." He paused. "Betcha you'd like it more than that silly wheel."

But Haley just spun more furiously on her wheel, not stopping to acknowledge his presence this time. She instead created the familiar whir that used to calm his frenzied mind. Robert left the room, and even though he was crying he surprised himself by hoping for a sunny day tomorrow. Maybe he'd take a walk in the park, or head to a show.

Numbers were just numbers, and he felt something new, something different calling for him.

Justice

The card of Justice is about balance and integrity. Using bad judgment for selfish desires leads to irresponsible decisions. In the end, the harsh scales of justice must be balanced.

Consequences
Carla Girtman

"Cookie! Here boy!" Justin whistled for his dog. Damn. Cookie must have wakened from his vampiric sleep before he did and there would be hell to pay if he didn't find him. Then Justin heard the child screaming.

By the time Justin had reached his dog, the vampire wolfhound was lapping up the last of the little girl's blood from her mangled face; her tiny body was savaged and drained. The rest of Justin's vampire clan were there, waiting.

"We could not save her, Justin," Vleda, the vampire clan leader, said. "You were warned when you sired your dog to remove it from our society. You chose to ignore that advice. Now this innocent is dead." She motioned to the others who took the dead child away.

"Long ago, the vampires of this clan declared children off limits to our hunger and swore to protect them, an oath you freely accepted when you joined us. Now you have jeopardized us all. If we are lucky, we may be able to cover this up as another pit bull attack."

With gloved hands, Vleda handed Justin two heavy silver chains. "You know what must be done."

Justin said nothing. There was no defense, no excuse that would save Cookie – or his own self.

Vleda chose a remote spot near the ocean ad watched as Justin pounded the stake into the ground anchoring the silver chains. Cookie howled as Justin snapped on of the chains around the wolfhound's neck. Smoke curled where the silver touched flesh.

I'm sorry, little buddy," he said stroking the dog's head, then fastened the other chain around his own neck. Justin ignored his pain and watched Vleda fade into the darkness.

Cookie whimpered, resting his head in Justin's lap. Together, they waited for the morning sun.

The Hanged Man

Martyrdom can be emblematic when The Hanged Man is reversed. However, this card also represents an ability to adapt to changing circumstances if one lets go of the ego

.

Resurrection

Megan Elizabeth Stafford

Maggie stood in front of the Holographic Robotics building and leaned on her cane, staring at the Holographic Robotics logo, a red circle with HR centered and flanked by angel wings. Below the logo were the words "Where dreams have wings." Some stranger with a white dog had handed her the card said that her journey was just beginning.

All she could see was the ending. The antigravity failure finished her career as a dancer three years ago. Even with the best medicine money could buy, it still could not give her back her fine-tuned muscles and only offered pain management. Pain which had become her constant companion and now her benefits with the ballet company were running out and she would have to have to go on government assistance if she didn't find something else soon.

Where dreams have wings. That's what the card said. That's what Holographic Robotics said it could offer her. Hope glimmered. Maybe, just maybe, they could help her. Maggie popped one of the several opioids she could take, climbed the three steps, and walked through the glass doors.

She could have just stepped into her living room, the room was so inviting. The walls, the color of rich cream, complemented the burgundy fabric couch and two matching side chairs which flanked a light oak accent table with a decorative bowl of fresh calla lilies, her favorite flower. Beneath the Oriental rug, the angled lines of the polished oak floor disappeared behind the receptionist's desk which could have been mistaken for a buffet table. There did not appear to be any doors other than the one she came through.

She approached the receptionist who smiled as though Maggie was the most important person to enter the room. Her blond hair spilled over a slender shoulder as she flickered ever so slightly. Maggie recognized the same holographic program that her plethora of doctors used. Disappointment welled within her.

"Welcome, I'm Traci," she said. Her head tilted, as though she were listening to an unheard voice. "Do you have an appointment?"

"No," she said. "Do I need one?"

"Not at all." Traci beamed hospitality. "May I have your name?"

Maggie was sure that the hologram had already gone through a photo database and knew exactly who she was, a has-been prima ballerina. Still it was nice she didn't make it obvious. "Margaret Starfire."

"Thank you, Ms. Starfire," she tilted her head, listening again, then straightened. "Marc will be out shortly. Would you care for something to drink while you wait? Water? Coffee? Tea?"

"Water would be lovely," she said.

Traci reached behind her and a bottle of water with Holographic Robotics winged logo appeared in her hand.

"Thank you." That was new. A hologram that could physically interact with a person. Technology was amazing, but not amazing enough, she thought as she accepted the proffered bottle.

"Please permit me to store your purse in our safe. This was you don't have to worry about losing it." Again, the warm smile. It was a polite way of saying the company couldn't allow bags or containers beyond reception.

"Of course." Maggie tucked the folding cane in her handbag and handed the purse to Traci. She still felt embarrassed that a woman her age had to use a cane.

She sat down on the plush couch and drained the small bottle of water not realizing how thirsty she was. And anxious. She leaned back against the couch, reveling in its comfort and thinking about how fast the opioid had gotten into her system. Usually it took far longer and only took the edge off. She stretched and curled her toes in her custom-made shoes. No pain shooting up through her feet. No pain in her left knee. She waggled her hips against the cushiony couch. No pain there either. Years of ballet discipline kept the tears from spilling over. For the first time in three years, she had no pain. She resisted the temptation to take another pill.

"Ms. Starfire?" A young man with dark curly hair, maybe in his thirties – it was so hard to tell these days with nanobots erasing age as fast as it appeared—entered the lobby carrying a green folder. Most people liked the age of the thirties: young enough to maintain an active life and old enough to be considered mature. It was the age Maggie herself liked the best, but even the nanobots could repair her body only so far. "I'm Marc."

"Please, call me Maggie." She hesitated before standing, not wanting to lose the delicious moment of being pain free.

"Are you all right?" Marc sat beside her. "Do you need me to call for medical assistance?"

"No," she said, smiling. "Must be the new drug the doctor gave me. I feel fine." She stood. "Better than fine."

"Wonderful," he said. He tapped the green folder in his hand. "Traci was able to pull up some information on you. I had no idea of your dancing talent."

"Not much of a talent now," Maggie said, feeling a warm flush creep up around her cheekbones.

"Nonsense. We can use that talent here at Holographic Robotics."

"How so?" Suspicion rankled Maggie. She had heard this kind of spiel from companies before. Promises that never panned out when they saw just how damaged she was.

"Follow me." Marc offered his hand to help her stand. "I can't wait to show you." His green eyes crinkled with excitement.

She accepted his assistance and limped beside him to the next room. Nanobots may have repaired her damaged left leg, but still left it about quarter inch short, adding a limp to her embarrassment of being defective. Marc didn't seem to notice. He touched a section of the blank wall which shimmered open revealing a cavernous room. Before her stood a robot with legs like tree trunks and feet the size of small dump trucks. One of its articulated arms held a massive sword, the other a shield.

"Meet the Black Knight."

"It sure is tall," she said, craning her neck, walking around it trying to figure out just how someone would climb in to operate it. "Looks hard to operate."

"Twenty, thirty years ago you would be right. But here at Holographic Robotics, we've overcome the hydraulic problem with our new patented human integration process that allows us to build these types of robots bigger, more flexible, and faster," Marc said. "We've been able to take it from a two-person to a one-person operation. Our company has revolutionized robotic combat."

Red flags of caution buzzed in her head. Robotic combat? Human integration? "What's that got to do with me?"

"Robotic combat is the money maker right now and we are looking to revolutionize the industry. We need people like you who have the memory skill to be the brains of our robots."

"Like me." Now she was being reduced to a combat robot. This was not how she wanted to entertain an audience.

Marc frowned. "No. We need you to help develop a program that can give people back their way of life. But that's going to take major funding. Combat robots are a way of making lots of money."

"So what do I have to do?" Red flags were still waving, but avoiding government assistance was crucial. There were a lot of things she didn't want to give up, but apparently dignity wasn't one of them.

"Simply download yourself into the robot brain," Marc told her. "Move around. Get a feel for how it moves."

"How much pain is involved?" Maggie asked.

"None," Marc reassured her. "That's the beauty of robotics. When you are in the robot, you aren't conscious of any pain." He laughed. "Even when you are being pounded into the ground. I should know." He waved a hand and a holographic video of a two robots fighting floated in midair. "That's me as the Black Knight fighting the Red Crusher." Marc winced as they watched the image of Red Crusher pummeling the Black Knight into a fetal position. "I wasn't very good at being a combatant." They both laughed.

"Want to try the Black Knight out? Just two minutes."

"Sure." What did she have to lose, meager government benefits? "What's first?" A sharp pinch like a thin needle shot through her hip, the first indicator her meds were losing strength.

Marc patted a dark gray chair and lifted a small helmet with dark gray visor. "Sit here," he said.

Maggie sank into the soft leather chair and it surrounded her body like a warm bubble bath. The needle pain in her hip subsided.

"Wow," she breathed, relaxing into the chair. "Can I take this home?"

He laughed. "It's going on the market next month. I'll make sure one's waiting for you when you get home."

"I'm sure I can't afford it," Maggie closed her eyes. She couldn't remember the last time she felt so comfortable. Marc placed the helmet on her head. Like the chair, it conformed itself into perfect comfort.

"Ready for the test drive?" His voice was muffled.

Maggie nodded.

His hand guided her hands to the indentions embedded in the arms of the chair and pressed her index finger gently.

A warm vibration tingled through her body and she opened her eyes. She stared down first at Marc who now looked like a small child barely reaching her robot knee. Then she saw herself.

I'm so frail, she thought and quickly looked away from the bone-thin woman cradled in the billowy gray chair. She staggered from a flash of vertigo and dropped the giant sword. Marc jumped out of the way as it clacked beside him.

"Take it slow," he said, his voice now echoed inside her head.

"Sorry," Maggie's voice boomed in her ears. She nodded, stooped to retrieve the sword, and then leaned it against the wall. She turned, moved, and flexed. The robot responded as though it were her own body. It was her body. A body without pain.

"You are doing really well. Now raise your right hand."

Maggie raised her right hand and the Black Knight raised its right hand. Marc had her run through a litany of exercises. Left step. Right step. Step up. Step down. Bend over. Squat down. Her actual body mimed every action.

"Now try to do it without moving your actual body."

She wanted to try more than that.

With face pointing to the ceiling, Maggie raised her right leg at a forty-five degree angle and rested her toe on her thigh. She curved her arms, palms down, over her head, like the ballerina on her antique music box. Using the robot's square foot as a ballet toe box, she stood on point with her left leg. She glanced at her body in the chair and noted that it was resting comfortably in a relaxed position with no signs of the ballet position she was holding. Exhilaration thrilled through her. A little clunky, but she could dance again.

"Bravo," said Marc. "I had no idea that robot could be so flexible." He touched the chair to disconnect her from the robot. "Time to rejoin the real world."

She gasped as she was pulled back into her own body. "That was two minutes? Can't I have a little more time?"

"Sorry. Safety reasons," he said, helping her out of the chair and guiding her gently to a table. "That was amazing. I have never seen anyone take to the integration system so well. Would you like to become part of the robotic combat circuit? You don't even have to win."

"Where do I sign?" she said, glancing back at the robot frozen in the ballet pose. Who needed the ballet company?

***

Maggie pirouetted around the ring of combat before her first match. She was beautiful. Trim, slender, and more graceful than the other robotic warriors, she looked every bit the frail dancer. She flirted with the first seat patrons, posed for pictures, holding the heaviest on one palm to demonstrate her strength. Marketing had done their job; there were no empty seats for the match of the century: The Ballerina versus The Red Crusher. When the match was over, The Red Crusher lay at her feet, one of its legs bent at an odd angle. She pirouetted around Crusher once, then stepped on its head grinding it into the hard-packed sand, soon to become her signature move.

The crowd chanted "Ballerina" over and over as Maggie basked in the adulation of her fans. Someone threw a bouquet of roses which The Ballerina caught in her huge hand. She made a show of smelling the tiny flowers and cupping them gently to her chest. She wished the Ballerina could smile at the crowd as she waved like a queen waving to her subjects. Energy rushed as the memory of her first opening night as prima ballerina spilled throughout her thoughts.

***

Maggie was sparring as the Ballerina in her back yard practicing new moves she had learned in martial arts class when Marc dropped by her lavish home carrying a green folder. He wasn't kidding. Robotic combat was a money maker. She had more money than she had dreamed possible. But he looked worried.

"Can I see you as you for a change?" he asked.

The Ballerina shrugged, crooked one large finger, and he followed the robot inside. There it anchored itself into its charging unit next to the comfort chair where Maggie sat snuggled. It hissed as it released her.

"You are looking a little thin," Marc said.

"The doctor says I'm fine," she said, wincing as she dropped into the oversized wingback chair. A nurse in a pale blue uniform handed her a couple of pills and a glass of water. Maggie gulped them down and nodded toward her. "She makes sure I take all my nutrients, monitors my pain meds, and get enough exercise. But she only lets me be the Ballerina two, maybe three, hours a day. If I had my way, I would never get out of her."

"We're all concerned," he said sitting opposite her. "We still don't know what all the long term effects are yet. We don't want you to become too dependent on the Ballerina's technology."

Maggie knew that was a lie. She knew her die-hard fans still loved her, but the media chatter was she had become too predictable. Even though she had never lost a match, it was only a matter of time before she did. She knew that too. The Red Crusher was aching for a revenge rematch. Judging from what she had seen, he would win this time. She knew Marc knew that too, but she wanted to see what he was going to offer her.

"Is that my new Ballerina contract?" She knew it wasn't, but the game had to be played.

"Different contract," Marc said, holding out the green folder. "Holographic Robotics wants Ballerina to retire while she's still on top."

Ice gripped her stomach. It was "retirement" from the ballet company all over again and time to move on. She ignored the green folder.

"What's going to happen to me then?" Maggie said. "Going to throw me on the ol' trash heap like the ballet company did? Ballerina's made a ton of money for the company."

"Nothing like that in the least," Marc said. "We still need you. That's what this contract is all about. The company is ready to explore a new way of download and wants you to test it. Are you open to that?"

"Will it be like Ballerina? Will I still move without pain?"

"Better," Marc said. "You can be anything or anybody."

Maggie didn't bother to read the contract as she scrawled a shaky signature across the bottom of it. At least she still had a job, pain medication, and place to live. She was, if nothing else, flexible.

Death

The Death card is not about dying but about transformation. When reversed, it is about loss or fear of change. Lost opportunity can be improved if one takes the time to chance it.

Death on Vacation

Aaron L. Garrison

"I'm sorry, sir," the TSA agent spoke. "You cannot carry on weapons."

"It must not leave my possession," snarled Death.

"Either surrender the weapon or check it at the airline desk. Next!"

He was dismissed. Death had been dismissed by a mere mortal. He gripped his scythe and trudged back to the check-in desk. In the old days he could have just smote that smug TSA agent. But no, the rules were different now. Death had to be compliant, friendly. Being on vacation meant he had to travel by air. Damn budget cuts. Instant teleportation was reserved for angels only.

"May I help you, sir?" said the airline agent. She was just a tiny bit too perky for Death.

"You told me I wouldn't have any problems taking this as a carry-on."

"No, Mr. Death. I said you could try to take it as a carry-on" she said, tapping into the computer and printing up a tag. That will be $129.95. Will that be cash, credit, or debit?"

"Yes, I need to check this." Death shoved his scythe toward her. "Am I going to miss my flight?"

"Oh, you shouldn't," "If you hurry, you shouldn't have any problems."

Her smile never flagged.

"It shouldn't cost me anything. You assured me that I could take it as a carry on."

"I cannot lose this. Can you guarantee it won't get lost?"

"Sir, it won't get lost."

"You've lost things before!"

"You could try changing it to a different shape, Mr. Death," a customer behind him said.

Death turned to see who had spoken. It was an older woman with a small white dog in her purse. A white silk rose was tucked in her pale blond hair that neatly framed her oval face. Faint laugh lines crinkled around blue eyes lending her a wise look in an otherwise unlined face.

The clerk laughed. "Please, Mr. Death. Will that be cash, credit, or debit?"

"Neither," he said. "I would like to rebook for a different flight."

"There is a change fee," she said, tapping into the computer.

"Of course there is."

Death turned back to the woman with the dog. "Thank you, my dear. That was a most helpful suggestion," Death said. "You may want to consider changing your flight. I think I have one last job to do."

"Oh I'm not on any flight," the woman with the dog said, flashing him a smile. "I just like standing in line."

"Here's your ticket, Mr. Death," said the clerk handing him a piece of paper. "Did you still want to check—"

Death waggled his hand at her. The scythe was now a stylish bracelet.

"Very nice, sir. Thank you for flying DelSpir."

Pocketing his ticket, he turned to offer to buy the woman a cup of coffee, but she had moved on to another line to entertain a child with her dog doing tricks.

Very enterprising, thought Death. That woman had opened all kinds of imaginative doors for him. He sighed. He might as well fly now. He couldn't get a refund, even if he wanted a refund. DelSpir was not known for its customer service. Pulling his ticket, he glanced at his departure time. Crap. He had to leave in 30 minutes and the security line was a mile long.

Death got in line behind a young Goth pushing his grandmother in a wheelchair.

"Sorry, sir," said an agent who was monitoring the lines. "This lane is for wheelchairs only. May I suggest the expert traveler lane?"

"But I only have 30 minutes to catch my plane. That line has over a hundred people."

"This is a wheelchair only lane, sir. Please select a different lane."

Death fell against the agent and into the Goth. Before the agent could recover, Death disappeared.

The agent stared at the silk screened image of Death waving farewell. The words "Don't Mess with Me" were emblazoned in red on the back of the Goth's black t-shirt. Death grinned. Vacations would be fun now.

Temperance

Life is full of ups and downs. A reversed Temperance can be a sign of conflict that can lead to an icy truce. But Temperance is strong, patient and kind, finding strength in the love thought lost.

Shadow of a Kiss
Gwendolyn Michaels

The words were out of his mouth before he could stop them. Ellana's sky blue eyes iced over. Copper hair flicked over her shoulder, brow furrowed, full lips pressed into a thin red line. David wanted to take it all back, everything, but it was too late. The kitchen door slammed followed by the car door banging shut. Standing at the bay window, he watched the Mercedes disappear down the tree-lined country driveway. Why didn't he just keep his thoughts to himself? She would return, he was sure of that. Her anger was like a summer storm: brief with rainbows.

David leafed through the yesterday's mail stacked on the oak table in the dining room. There was a postcard announcing the book signing at their local bookstore, the same bookstore where Ellena had completed her first book and had her book signing.

The doorbell rang. It was FedEx delivering two boxes, one large and one small. He signed for them and set them on the table. The larger box was from her publisher, probably her usual ten copies of her new book. He opened the smaller one. It was the Waterman Carene Blue Obsession fountain pen he had ordered for her as an anniversary surprise for the upcoming book signing. He put the pen in his pocket and picked up the postcard announcement to read it again. The book signing was today at two.

He slumped in his seat and opened the other box and took out a book, nearly dropping it. There on the cover was the watercolor portrait he had sketched of her sitting in her leather wingback chair writing with her favorite pen: head bowed, right leg tucked underneath, a shoe dangling from her left foot, and her untouched tea sitting on the table next to the silver tea service, a neglected wedding gift. The late afternoon sunlight filtered through the lace curtains scattering gold highlights to her coppery hair in fiery halo. A wide lock of hair fell across her face as she wrote, obscuring her features. The wall behind her was in shadow; their wedding portrait washed nearly invisible in its darkness. The title of her book "I Only Kiss Your Shadow" was scripted in a stylized font.

She had never told him she was using his art as her cover. David, pleased and surprised to see his artwork on the cover, opened the book and turned to the dedication page. *To my beloved: Without you, I am but a shadow on the wall.* Was he her beloved? Based on events of the last year, he wasn't sure. But seeing his artwork displayed on the cover, gave him a tiny something he didn't want to call hope.

David arranged the books into two stacks on the table. Slipping the pen from his pocket, he put an ink cartridge in it and pulled out his ever-present sketchbook to make sure the pen wrote smoothly. He etched some lines, creating an audience with standing room only. As he continued to add more detail, he wished he had ordered another pen for himself. He glanced up and there, hanging in the air, like a delicate hologram, was his sketch in full animated color. Behind the holographic audience, Ellena entered the room smiling and shaking hands with everyone who reached for her. He saw himself give her the pen and greet her with a kiss.

He looked down at his blue and white sketch. The sketch of the audience was there, but not her or him. He looked back up, but the hologram was gone. Holding up the pen, he twirled it around examining it from all angles.

He remembered the first time he met Ellena at waterfront in San Francisco trying to sell his art. She stood before his watercolor, "Fishing at Sunrise," with a well-loved book in her hand. In his sketchbook, he had already captured the pensive look on her face, the way she held one slender finger as a bookmark, and how her copper hair was held captive in a crocheted snood at the back of her neck. His colored pencils highlighted the sun's gold threads as they wound their way around the tiny fiery curls that framed her oval face sprinkled with a dust of freckles. It was her pensive face moving from book to painting that encouraged him to speak to her.

"What do you think of the painting?" he asked.

"It's just like Emily Dickinson's poem *The Sea of Sunset,*" she said, reciting the short poem in a breathy way he found charming.

"The painting is called *Fishing at Sunrise*." David was amused at her analogy.

"Well, you have named it wrong," she declared, tossing her hair back in a flirtatious way. "It should be called *The Sea of Sunset*."

"Very well," he laughed. "Consider it renamed."

It was his only sale of the day for she had stolen his heart.

Ellena still had not returned home. David used the pen sketch as a guide for a watercolor painting. Using a soft pencil, he outlined Ellena sitting in a blue velvet wingback chair, leaning forward against the table as she wrote her name in her book for a woman whose expression held repressed excitement. Between her fingers was a ticket with the number 1. In the background stood several other customers exchanging conversations as they held their books waiting their turn. One man, third in line, was already reading the book with a faint smile. Farther back in the line, stood a young mother distracting her little boy with a stuffed bear. The manager was at the cash register taking a teenager's money in the far back of the store.

Satisfied with the detailed moment, he added the watercolors bringing the painting to life. He then set the painting aside on the dining room chair to dry.

He was in the kitchen preparing the kettle for tea, when he heard the front door open.

"When did you do this?" she said.

"Don't touch. It's still wet," he called from the kitchen. "I did it while you were out."

"You weren't there? The painting is amazing," she said, joining him in the kitchen. "It's exactly what happened."

"Do you like it?" He had handed her a cup that was in their wedding pattern, a delicate lace design etched in Dresden blue, her favorite color. The pattern she had picked out. He also set out some shortbread cookies. Tea and cookies – this was how they always celebrated their anniversary.

"Very much," she said, taking a sip. Her eyes closed and the corners of her mouth turned up. "You always know how to brew an excellent cup of Darjeeling."

She didn't even notice the china pattern or the shortbread.

He poured another cup of tea in a matching cup, stirred in two sugars and sat across from her. After ten years, he had expected a little more romance than this. The afternoon sun crept through the kitchen door window putting Ellena into silhouette as she sat at the table.

"How did the book signing go?"

"They are always fun," she replied. "Are you sure you weren't there? It's eerie how accurate the painting is."

She got up and he followed her into the dining room.

Ellena pointed at the painting. "Right down to the mother with the little boy and his bear."

David didn't tell her about the hologram. They stood a moment in front of the painting and then sat down in the wingback chairs facing each other; a wordless emptiness hung between them.

Ellena turned back to the painting. "I like the way you captured the light and shadow to give it an air of expectation. Reminds me of –"

"One of Emily's poems?"

"Not this time," she laughed. "I was thinking of Norman Rockwell." She took another sip of tea. "Remember the hours we spent debating who was the better poet, Robert Frost or Emily Dickinson?" she sighed.

"I loved those arguments," he said, studying his tea as he swirled it in lazy circles not wanting to meet her eyes. "Even if Emily always won."

"I remember how your eyes changed from green to brown that day we met," she said.

"But my favorite memory was when I found your ring in a nearly impossible to find 1924 edition of her collected poems," she said it so softly he almost didn't catch it.

The shadow of evening spilled through the bay window as they sat sipping their tea. Once the two of them had so much in common. They could talk for hours about their hopes and their dreams. Now that they had it all, they could barely hold a conversation without it drifting into banality. When did their lives become so different? He sighed. Turning his cup round in his hand, he noticed a hairline crack down its side. He placed the cup gently in the sink. Maybe a second honeymoon on a cruise would rekindle their romance.

Behind him, he heard the clink of a cup as Ellena set hers inside his. His cup did not break.

"Darling, let's eat out tonight," she suggested, draping her arms around his shoulders. "And celebrate."

He barely felt her lips against his cheek, a shadow of a kiss.

He wasn't certain what they were celebrating, their anniversary or her book. But it didn't matter. They were still together.

"Sure," he said.

The Devil

Motive figures strongly with The Devil card which deals with greed and power, and ignorance can be a trap if signs are ignored. It has always been said "don't count your chickens before they are hatched" or in this case cockroaches

The Client

Carla Girtman

I was on notice. With the economy sinking and stock market tanking, I was supposed to bring in five new clients or find employment elsewhere. I boarded the train, found a private compartment, slid into a faux leather seat, and thumbed through appointments for tomorrow on my smart phone. Nothing. Not one appointment. No leads either. I sighed and slipped the phone back into my pocket. Everyone I knew was either broke or asking me for a job. Investment counseling is not the money-maker everyone thinks it is. I slumped in my seat wondering how was going to break the news to my wife as the train lurched forward.

A winged cockroach, about the size of my thumb, scurried in under the door and climbed up beside me. If it wasn't for the fact he was dressed in overalls and a tee shirt, I would have squashed him right there.

"Hey, is this seat taken?" it asked in a louder voice than I had expected.

"No," I said, resisting my urge to crush it. I stared out the window watching the thunderheads gather in the blackening sky. Crap. It would be raining when I got home. And me with no umbrella. Perfect way to end the day.

"Thanks." It flung its tiny lunchbox on the seat across from me, fluttered over, and took a seat. "Been dodging newspapers and shoes since I got on board."

Talking cockroaches – who knew. I put aside my aversion for creepy-crawlies. Opportunity knocked at strange doors and I needed to open this one. If he could talk and hold down a job, perhaps this could be a break for me.

"Can I buy you a drink?" I asked. "You look like you've had a hard day." Establish rapport – lesson one to creating a new client.

"That's nice of you, man. Thanks. I'll just have a capful of whatever you're having." I swiped my card in the refrigerator slot and pulled out an imported beer. I stopped thinking of him as an insect and poured a capful for my new client.

"I'm Gary Sweatson," I said. "What's your name?"

"Jacks –short for Jackson. Most of my people only have first names." Jacks' head dipped into the twist off cap, smiling as only a cockroach can smile. "That tastes great." He kicked up all his legs, crossing the bottom two. "I'll tell ya what. Working to feed a thousand hungry mouths is a killer. Got kids?" "

No, we might be expecting." I lied. Lesson two – create common ground.

"Tough break. Mine's always expecting."

We laughed.

I tipped my bottle in my mouth, letting the smooth amber liquid cool my dry throat. I couldn't believe I was working a cockroach to become a client. Outside, rain pelted the window. The reflection of a woman with a white rose in her hair hung momentarily on the window. I heard a yap of a small dog and the jingle of small bells go by. The reflection vanished and a business card slide under the compartment door. I picked it up and read "Fool's Party Planner and Catering." Another potential client, I thought. Things seemed to be looking up.

"Haven't seen you on the train before. New in town?" I asked, sitting down and tucking the business card in my pocket.

"Naw," Jacks, the cockroach, replied. "Had to give up my car. Gas getting too expensive."

I suppressed a smile. It was hard to imagine a such a tiny car on the freeway.

"Me too." I lied. "What do you do?"

"Troubleshooter. Go into a building, find poisons, warn the tenants. How about you?"

"Investor."

"Awesome." His antennae twitched. I wondered if he was interested, but I stayed cool. Lesson three – don't seem eager. "What'd you think of last night's game?" I asked.

"Disappointing. Lost money on that one."

"Yeah, me too.

We sat in silence until the train screeched to a halt. "This is where I get off," I said. "It's been nice talking to you." I didn't care that it was still raining. I could see my wife's car in the parking lot waiting for me, so I wouldn't get too wet.

"Nice meeting you." Jacks, the cockroach, extended a leg to shake my hand. "Hey, I'm in the market for a new broker. Can I come in some time to review my investment portfolio?"

"Sure," I said, handing him a business card, making a mental note to have smaller ones printed. I pulled out my phone and tapped Jacks' name into my calendar. "What time is good for you tomorrow?" I wondered how many friends he had and called my secretary to give her a heads up.

The next morning I called "Fools Party Planner and Catering," and got voicemail. I left my number and a promise to call back later in the afternoon. Jacks was due in around 10. The intercom buzzed.

"Gary," it was my secretary. "Mr. Handel wants to see you."

I walked into my boss' office. I wanted to give him the good news about my new client.

"Gary," Handel said. "I'm going to have to let you go. Jacks here is taking your place. He's bringing the firm about five thousand new clients."

Jacks, dressed in a three-piece suit, and touched the tip of his antennae in a salute and smiled his cockroachy grin.

Lesson four—never trust a cockroach. I should have squashed him when I had the chance.

The Tower

Losing a loved one can send even the strongest person into despair. The Tower can signal that it is time to reevaluate life circumstances, but making changes do not always lead to a happy ending.

Immortality

Megan Elizabeth Stafford

Forever together was our promise

Of a life filled with bliss.

But lightning struck our tower wall

From the window I fall and fall.

My world explodes: and you are gone.

Crippled, alive and alone

I read on that cold slab of stone

Your name, your birth, your death.

Tears flow down. With painful breath

I leave with you one white rose.

Down the path I wander alone.

Bright and cheery, the sunlight shone

But finds no way to my unhappy heart.

Resigned forever we are apart.

I wish for your life, not mine.

As my habit I spend the day
Where my love and life lay
Buried beneath verdant sod.
Heavy lies my head. I shroud
Bitter tears behind my hands.

A step before me did I hear linger
And through a hedge of fingers,
I see a stranger, her smile sweet.
With a voice of silk, she speaks,
"Why do you walk among the dead?"

A torrent of words spilled and tumbled.
The crash, the fire, the ground that rumbled,
and rage of water in a flash
swept my love from my grasp.
I could do nothing but call her name.

Hollow, empty, grief all spent,
Anger gone, the ache now absent.
On her shoulder, my head rests
I hear her words; my soul they test.
"We can bring your love back to you."

"Work for us," she said. Her promise golden
Ripples through my mind, desire unfolding.
"You know of anger, how sadness smothers.
Knowing those things can you aid others,
she spoke. May the gods forgive me, I listened.
For many I now bring happiness, contentment.
To those who wander through the maze of torment
Encourage and comfort, I play the part
Guiding the lost and wayward heart
To the place of happiness they want most.

A fool with a dog who does his tricks,
Traveling companion with knapsack and stick.
Mother, father, sister, brother,
Fairy, warrior, moonlight lover,
I am what they need me to be.

Their sadness captured and confined
At day's end, when their grief is mine,
I cleanse my soul beside the sea.
By the shore she waits for me.
Together we sit until night comes.

Her hand holds mine, our fingers lock

Words unspoken, no need for talk.

I feel her kiss, but know the lie.

She is no more real than I.

The Star

Children are the future, but it is uncertain where their paths may lead. Change can be unsettling, but should be met with joy a vision of tomorrow. Even when reversed, The Star suggests staying the course, even when distractions threaten misdirection.

Baby Heaven

Gwendolyn Michaels

I summoned a robo-taxi.

"Everything will be fine, Janine," I said, guiding my wife into the taxi. I swiped my credit card and chose "closed to others" option. It was more expensive, but I wanted Janine to have privacy. There was no need to share our despair with other riders. Besides, we could always afford it.

I sat opposite of Janine who curled up on her seat, clutching her pocketbook like it was a life preserver. She struggled to blink back yet another disappointment. I reached over to brush away the one tear that got away.

"Confirm closed to others?" asked the taxi.

"Confirm," I said. I always found the voice of taxis disconcerting. Technology was always trying to find a way of being human. It should focus on something important like solving the world's infertility problem, not sounding like some patronizing smooth-voiced woman.

"Destination?"

I hesitated. Janine and I had been on a waiting list for over twelve years. Even the black market couldn't find children. I watched Janine trying to bury her sadness behind a scrunched linen handkerchief. The doctor had filled us with such hope this time. What should I do? Return home to a house with a room full of unboxed reminders of children who will never be? Or go somewhere else? Somewhere questionable. I wanted only Janine's happiness.

"Destination?" the robo-voice chimed. "Fifteen seventy-two Wilson Avenue, Angels Hollow."

"The destination is approximately 50 miles north of New Los Angeles outside city limits and will take twenty minutes by air or one hour thirty minutes by street level."

"By air, please."

"Press thumbprint to accept additional air charge."

"We will be there soon," I promised, moving over to sit beside Janine, sliding one arm around her slim shoulders. she laid her head against my shoulder, her herbal shampoo scent filling my nose. The taxi glided up and sped forward, Los Angeles melting into a distant green patchwork quilt crosshatched with silver ribbons.

***

I instructed the hovering robo-taxi to wait fifteen minutes. If we needed to escape, well, we'd be ready. The building's facade reminded me of a lavish hotel that Janine and I had honeymooned in Switzerland twelve years ago. Waterfalls, spilling from just below the rooftop of the building overhang, flanked the heavy glass doors. Each waterfall had a Romanesque style statue which sat near an infinity pool, left foot in the water. The woman, her nudity artfully obscured by her hair and the pitcher she held, added water to the infinity pool whose edge disappeared somewhere beneath the building. I watched the waterfalls gush from the ceiling's edge, finding the sound of the water almost hypnotic. The doorman opened one of the heavy glass doors and we stepped inside.

Inside was different. The lobby was airy and spacious. Moving images of babies of different ethnicities, sizes, and ages filled the large television monitors. Glass boxes held rotating holographic older children models. It could have been a car dealership.

"Do you think this is the only way, Matt?" asked Janine. She stared at one of the monitors where a yellow-capped fool performed magic tricks at a party. He pulled a white rose from the ear of one of the delighted children.

"We can leave any time you want."

"Hello," a woman greeted us. Her name tag said "Barbara" and she reminded me of my grandmother. "Welcome to Baby Heaven. How can we be of assistance?"

Janine blushed. "We want to make the parental step," she said, "but—" she hesitated not wanting to go into detail.

"It's both of us," I said, maybe too loudly. "The tests showed we couldn't produce any children."

"So many of us have that problem," the woman said, clasping Janine's hand and giving it a pat. "But here at Baby Heaven everyone can be a parent. We even offer older models for those parents don't want to go through the baby stage."

"Where does Baby Heaven get its children?" I asked. I had done my homework ever since I had heard about Baby Heaven. I had even interviewed parents and did a rigorous investigation. Nothing. Not even the Net with all its fingers in everyone's lives could find anything negative to say. For me, that in itself was a red flag. But Janine – well, babies were on her mind a lot.

"Well, we don't steal children or kidnap pregnant women," Barbara said, "despite what you may have heard. We have our special baby process."

"Are the children real?" Janine whispered.

"Oh mercy, yes," the woman said. "Let me show you and put your minds at ease."

Janine and I followed Barbara through double glass doors into a hospital nursery. We stopped in front of a large window to admire the twenty or so babies sleeping in glass enclosed bassinets. "Aren't they the cutest?"

Janine put her hand on the window, leaning for a closer look, breath fogging the glass pane. "Can we take one home today?"

"Oh my, I wish I could say yes," Barbara said, "but these babies already have parents. They are just waiting for delivery day."

"What about the babies who don't turn out right and parents change their minds?" Janine whispered. "What happens to them?"

"Oh, honey child," Barbara smiled. "All our children are wanted."

"How long does it take?" I asked.

"Nine months, like any baby. The first step is to take a DNA sample from each parent. It's just like if you were making your own baby. We combine your DNA in our special process to produce a child. No court could take a DNA sample from one of our babies to prove it wasn't human."

"Oh, Matt," Janine whispered, squeezing my hand. "It's perfect."

It had been months since I had seen her so happy.

"Shall we start the paperwork?" Barbara asked.

***

"Picture time," Janine giggled, holding the two babies in her lap.

I laughed and framed my family in the viewfinder and snapped a picture. I stared at the digital picture in disbelief. There was Janine crisp and clear, arms curved like she was holding the children, but no babies. Looking through the viewfinder, I saw the children and Janine. I clicked again. No children. I deleted the pictures, "accidentally" dropped the camera, shattering it.

"Clumsy me," I said, stroking my children's fuzzy heads, hair soft under my fingers. Yes, of course they were real. "I'll get a new camera tomorrow."

"It's OK," she said to me. "Time for naps."

What was it Barbara had said about taking pictures? I couldn't remember. My stomach churned as I dialed Baby Heaven's number.

The Moon

When The Moon makes an appearance in a tarot spread, it can foretell unexpected possibilities as well as indicate deceit and lies – which may not always be a bad thing.

Standing on Gravity's Edge

Genevieve Worthington

Dorian listened to Javed's even breathing as he lay asleep. Both were naked in his bed barely wide enough for them both. The last year or so she had taken to sleeping in his quarters rather than her own just to be with him. Who would have thought she would find the love of her life in space?

Javed turned on his side with a sigh and she slid against him, spoon fashion, with her chest to his back. She took comfort in his muscled strength, feeling the strong thud of his heart and felt safe.

***

She met Javed the first day she had arrived on the freighter, the *Luna's Tune*. He had brought in two dead crew members and stowed them in the refrigerator unit that was bigger than her office.

"You must be the new doc," he said. "Sorry to start your first day off like this." He stuck out his hand, square and muscular. "I'm Javed."

"Dorian," she said. Her heart thumped as she accepted his proffered hand. She felt faint, giddy, and breathless all at once. It brought to mind the time when she ten and stood transfixed in the middle of Grand Canyon Skywalk, a transparent horseshoe bridge, fearful she would plummet to river four thousand feet below. Dorian released her grip on his hand and her breath she had been holding. "I guess I'd better get to work."

As medical officer, part of her job was to harvest bodies for transplantation, another form of salvage for the Company to make money. All employees, per their contracts, were automatic organ donors.

"They're not going anywhere," Javed said, his smile warm and generous. He slipped his arm around her waist and guided her out the door. "Come on. Let me show you around the ship."

***

She lay on her back counting the rivets in gray-green ceiling, something she did when she couldn't get right to sleep. More rivets were missing. God. The

Company wouldn't spend a farthing on any repair unless it could make money from it. And the recovery operations, as the Company was fond of calling them, were getting more dangerous. In the past year, there had not been one salvage where somebody didn't die. Tomorrow Javed would go out with his crew to "recover" an abandoned space station. Anything could go wrong. She hugged him tight.

"What?" Javed said sleepily. He turned to face her. She teetered on the edge of the bed until he flung an arm around her, pulling her close. "Ready for another go round?" He cupped her face, his lips finding hers, then sliding down her neck, and breasts.

"I had a bad dream about tomorrow's salvage," Dorian said, responding to his caresses with her own. "I'm scared for you. All of you."

"Shh," he said. "You worry too much," he said, running his fingers through her hair. "Everything will be fine."

She shivered under his gentle touch as his fingers followed the curve of her spine and rested on her bottom. "It's just a routine salvage operation."

It was anything but routine. The crew stowed today's casualty, body mangled beyond recognition in the chiller for organ processing. Dorian closed the chiller door and rested her forehead against it, letting its metal surface cool her hot face.

"You OK, Doc?" It was Carl, Javed's second in command. His hand rested on her shoulder.

She did not shrug off his hand, only nodded, not daring to speak or move.

"Javed was a good man. He saved us all," he said, giving her shoulder one last squeeze before letting her go. "Join us at Gravity's Edge and lift your glass one last time."

"Thanks, Carl," she said. "I'll be all right."

"You sure?" he asked. "You haven't been planet-side in weeks. We miss you."

"Got a lot to do, Carl," Dorian said. "It's not like I risk my life doing my job."

"Sure, Doc," Carl said. "We'll save you a save a chair. Just in case."

"Sure. Just in case," she whispered. Tears slipped down her face. The door opened and closed.

She stepped inside the chiller, sat down beside Javed, and wept until there was nothing left except a dull heartache.

Her tears were spent, there was nothing left to do but harvest the body parts, something she had done a hundred times. Her hand shook as her scalpel poised over his chest. The room swam and spun all at once, that giddy sensation of near falling, just like the first time she had to harvest. She grabbed the edge of metal table in white-knuckled grip.

"I can't do this," she whispered and her vision wavered. Then she remembered his words the first time she had to harvest one of the crew.

"Sure you can," he said. "It's just a hologram."

***

Dorian entered the Gravity's Edge—bubbling with voices and the heady scent of ale reminding her of an English pub—and saw the Carl waving frantically from the corner of the room. There were at least twenty crew members with him.

"Hey, Doc! You made it," Carl called out. "Saved ya a seat."

Someone ordered her an ale and shoved it in her hand.

"To Javed," someone else said. "Who always said 'never leave a mate behind' and 'never leave a woman wanting more.' "

Dorian laughed for the first time in days, and raised her glass joining the chorus to Javed's memory.

Another round of ale came.

"To Javed's wife," Carl said, raising his glass. "Doc Dorian."

Carl caught her glass without spilling a drop of ale. He winked at her. From his pocket he pulled out a simple gold band and slipped it on her finger. "Approval came through today. He was going to surprise you."

"I don't remember getting married," Dorian blurted out. She loved Javed, but they had never spoken about marriage.

"Javed married you the first day you came on board," Carl said, "He loved the cut of your jib." He winked again, raising his tankard of ale.

Everyone roared and raised their glasses.

"Now that you are married, you can't work for the Company. Some kind of nepotism rule," Carl pulled her out of her seat. "Come on. You got a flight to catch."

Dorian staggered to her feet. Heat flooded her face and the world spun around her. The alcohol sloshed and churned in her stomach, threatening to make an exit.

"I got you," Carl said sliding a strong arm behind her and lifting her off her feet.

She closed her eyes and let darkness overtake her.

Next thing she knew was waking up in the passenger seat of a luxury cruise ship. Carl had said something about catching a flight, but the details were fuzzy. Her head pounded and her stomach was queasy. How much had she had to drink? She looked at her left hand. Yes, there was the gold wedding ring. At least she remembered that part. Dorian looked up at the ceiling and counted the rivets. Not a single one missing.

Someone next to her, a man she thought, stirred awake. "You still count rivets to go to sleep?" he asked.

"How—?" Dorian turned and looked at the man. "Javed?" She wanted to sit up, but fell back head was still spinning. "But you're dead."

"As far as the Company knows, I am," he grinned. "And so are you. The *Luna's Tune* blew up shortly after the crew went planet side for some R and R. The company will be sending their condolences and handsome insurance payout to your identical twin sister on Centari."

"But I don't have –" Dorian said, then looked at Javed, understanding dawning.

"I've always fancied the name Sheila," he said, lacing his fingers in hers.

In the world of tarot, The Sun is one of the best cards to have appear. Although when in reverse it can be a signpost for delays or failure, knowing that someone is in your corner when the going gets tough can signal happy times.

Reality Check
Gwendolyn Michaels

With a headache pounding at the back of her head and every muscle proclaiming the flu had arrived, Ina Kalikasan shuffled into the kitchen. This was not the way she wanted to start her day. Maybe she just needed some tea. She put on the kettle.

While the water heated, she pulled on her oversized robe that hung on the dining room chair and shoved her feet into fuzzy pink slippers to get the morning paper. The air had the cool touch of winter with the promise of spring, and felt good against her hot skin. Damn. Feverish too. Maybe she should call in sick.

The ring on her left hand felt heavy as she reached for the morning paper. A touch of vertigo swirled her vision when she saw two black horse hooves and a white muzzle tearing up bites of her winter rye lawn.

She saw a golden horn between the horse's eyes as she met its gaze. A unicorn. Grazing on her lawn. The unicorn's eyes widened in surprise and she swore she heard it gasp.

"Good morning, my queen," said the unicorn, kneeling on one knee, touching its velvety lips to her bejeweled finger. "The signs of spring are at hand." With one last nibble from her lawn, the unicorn trotted around the corner of the house.

"What?" Ina followed, but the unicorn had vanished. Not so much as a footprint was left. Confused, she peeked around the corner one last time before going back to the kitchen.

The kettle whistled and she poured the water over the green tea in the giant ceramic mug which proclaimed "I was royalty in a former life." A slice of whole wheat bread popped up in the toaster. She settled in her cushioned chair to read the paper.

THE SIGNS OF SPRING ARE AT HAND the headline trumpeted. She blinked, rubbed her eyes, and looked again. Now the headline read PRESIDENT SIGNS GRANT FOR AHHA."

First unicorns and now changing headlines? The day was getting weird. Again came that nagging need to remember something important. Something about gods? Being a god? She reached for her phone to call out sick and stopped. What was a phone? Did she even have a job? She couldn't even remember name. Taking some deep breaths, she quelled the panic that prickled. Then a wave a nausea churned her stomach and the walls crushed in around her. The headache nudged the back of her head. The ring weighed on her hand. What was with this stupid ring? She shoved the questions out of her mind. She needed to get out. Fresh air; that's what she needed.

It was a perfect day for a walk. A puffy cloud scudded across the sun dimming its brightness just enough for visual comfort. The light, cool breeze brushed against her face. Yes, outside was just what the doctor ordered. Her bathrobe had changed to a sweater and her fuzzy slippers to walking shoes. She decided she was in a pleasant dream and continued walk. No need to panic now that she knew she was in a dream.

The longer she walked, the more the scenery around her wavered from suburbia to forest and back again. The sidewalk transmogrified from concrete to a grassy path.

The manicured lawns lining the sidewalk had a strange sparkle about them, like an aurora borealis. A blond man in a harlequin shirt and black pants, walking a white dog with a jingling fool's cap, nodded as he strode by. Fairies of every size flitted about, twittering tinkly laughs and gave her tiny curtsies. Graceful elves from different mythic cultures bowed their heads in reverence as they glided by her on the grassy path. Huge winged gargoyles looped lazily in and out of the clouds.

Giddiness tickled her stomach and a buzzing sensation flooded her as the ring fell off her hand. The aurora sparkled and expanded around her. She stood in a forest. Her forest. Her home. She remembered everything. The wall between the two realities, human and fae, could be crossed once again—at least by the fae. Even more pressing, fae could no longer ignore the human impact on both realities.

A dryad, her face a pale nut brown, paced next to a willow tree wringing her hands.

"Phoebe," Gaia called. "I'm back."

Phoebe smiled and even her tree's willow branches waved with happiness. "Gaia, I was getting so worried. What happened? You were gone so long."

Gaia sat down on a branch which curved into an ornate, living chair. "The ring causes some memory and health problems, but they aren't serious. We have to hurry."

"But do we have allies in the human world?"

"Of course, dear one," Gaia smiled. "More than enough."

Judgment

Judgment represents rebirth and resurrection when revealed, but also a need to let go of the past. But if you cannot face the reality of your nature and make decisions to change, wounds can never heal as mermaids often find out.

Night of the Mermaid

Megan Elizabeth Stafford

Jeff was teaching me to drive a stick shift in the abandoned Mermaid Cemetery. With all its narrow, curvy roadways, it was the perfect place to learn to drive. It was also the place for lovers to make out among the huge boulders. The moon was full; the night air was filled with the ocean's breeze. Tonight was going to be special.

"Now, ease up on the clutch just as you are pressing the gas," Jeff said, his strong fingers curled around mine as I gripped the stick shift.

The Mustang bucked and stalled.

"I'm never going to get this," I muttered.

"Sure you will," he said, pressing his hand against mine as he guided it to shift in reverse. "See? Just got to press down and shift back."

His deep voice conjured the memory of the night he and I met at the Starlight Club.

***

"Where are you from?" The timbre of his voice was deep, strong, powerful – the type of voice I was always drawn to. He had two drinks in his hand and gave me one.

I took a tiny sip from the triangular stemmed glass. It was bitter. I remembered thinking it was good that it was bitter; that way I could keep it in my hand and pretend to drink it. Ordering something I didn't like was a good way to keep from drinking too much and staying in control.

"Everywhere and nowhere," I answered. "Navy brat." It was an answer I had learned from one of the movies I had seen in high school. General enough to keep people from asking too much without being rude. Kept me out of a lot of trouble in college. I stared at the clubbers gyrating on the dance floor. Energy flowed and I wanted to be with them.

"You look like you have lost your best friend," Jeff said. "Did he leave you for someone else?"

I smiled giving him kudos for a new pick up approach. I shrugged "No, not with anyone. Just wanting to be part of the action." I took another sip of my bitter drink. "Hey, you didn't just drug me, did you?"

Jeff looked panicked. "No. No!" he stammered. "I just noticed you were drinking a martini earlier and thought you might like a fresh one. You've been sitting there quite a while."

I laughed. "Let's dance," I said. "It's way more fun than drinking martinis."

He let me drag him into the crowd bouncing to the thunderous, thumping music. We bumped hips and I skimmed my fingers across his face. He pulled me close, our lips nearly touching. I could almost taste his dirty martini, the scent of olive brine hovered on his lips. His eyes, warm pools of hazel, made me feel I was the only one there. The dancers' energy washed over me like a tidal wave, and I fed off it like a vampire draining a willing victim.

***

Legend had it that in the time when true magic was practiced, mermaids were given the choice of having true love or immortality. Mermaids chose immortality, but at a cost. Every one hundred years, mermaids would join the human race and become human long enough to mate with a man. However, at the point when a mermaid was willing to give up her immortality in return for the love of a man, her kiss would turn the human to stone. As their lovers turned to stone, the mermaids wept tears of stone that now created the beige pebble coastline along the edge of Mermaid Cemetery.

Mermaid Cemetery was filled with black boulders that were scattered about like so many misshapen dominoes. Some stood erect, nearly as tall as Jeff, with carved shoulders, arms, legs, and feet. Others were supine and flat while others lay in a fetal position. Others mounded against the ocean shore. None had faces or perhaps if they had, those faces had been worn away by the weather. At least that's I thought what they looked like. But none of this mattered to me. Even if I believed it was true, I didn't love Jeff. I would never love him. It wasn't in my nature. All I wanted was the experience of giving myself totally to him.

Witching hour was near. I pulled over to our favorite secluded spot near the water's edge.

"There's a lunar eclipse tonight," Jeff said, draping an arm around me. "One of those goofy new agers at the university said the stars are in a special alignment."

"It's the night of the mermaid," I said settling into the crook of his arm. "when all mermaids must return to the ocean until the next celestial alignment."

"Oh right. And legend says any man who loves a mermaid turns to stone." He laughed. "If you believe any of that," he said. "Come on, let's go for a swim. I'm hot." Jeff gave me a sly wink.

"OK." I returned his wink, slipping out of everything but the bikini underneath. That wasn't going to stay on long either because I was hot too. "Catch me if you can."

It was nearly midnight. A full moon crept over the ocean casting an eerie light onto the boulders. Jeff chased me around a few boulders before catching me near one of the bigger stones. His eyes glittered in the moonlight like chips of amber gold. His lips were warm against mine. As he held me tight, his muscles strong, warm, and solid. I pressed into him. The cold water pulsing around our bare feet sent threads of electricity through me.

I slid from his arms and swam into deeper water about chest high. I shed the bikini, holding the top part waving it like a flag. He reached me in seconds, scooping me up. His mouth was hungry for mine as he ran strong fingers down my back and around my bottom. Lifting me up and pulling me close, I wrapped my legs around him and settled into his manhood. He rested my back against one of the large boulders poking out of the waist high water.

The water churned around us. His mouth found its way to my breasts nuzzling me like a suckling child teasing my nipples erect. He moved against me, pressing me against the cool rock. Unbidden, my back arched as his powerful thrusts sent fire throughout my body. It was unlike anything I had ever felt: fire, electricity, and happiness surging at the same time. I screamed as I felt his offering pour into me with one final thrust. We untangled and stood a moment, exhausted and exhilarated, letting the ocean swirl its cleansing water around us.

Jeff cupped my breasts, his lips and tongue caressing first one and then the other. His hands slid down my waist, then my hips where my fish tail began. It was all I could do to stay upright as he pushed me away.

"What the hell are you?" Jeff staggered back, his eyes wide with horror, words sluggish and distorted. "What have you done to me?" He struggled to get back to shore, but his flesh was already transmuting into stone, making it impossible to move. I cringed as his screams of agony pierced the sound of crashing waves. He became one of the fallen domino boulders along the shore line.

My tears, first hot liquid, became cold stone. One by one they plinked into the pulsating water, floating a moment before sinking beneath the wave. I fell against the boulder that once was Jeff and listened until his screams fell silent.

I cradled the Jeff-shaped rock, feeling his final warmth leach into the cold ocean waves. My tail whisked against the stony piles of tears heaped under the water around the boulder, stones I and others had left century after century.

"The legend says it's not when a man loves a mermaid," I wept, "but when a mermaid loves a man."

"I'm sorry." I sat with my fish tail curled around the boulder that once was Jeff until the sky turned pearly amethyst with the dawn. Tears now spent, I kissed him one last time before I returned to the comfort of my ocean.

While the flip side can warn of stagnation and delays, The World card can indicate success and fulfillment can be within reach. Even for zombies.

I Fall to Pieces

Seth Nelsen Bingham

Lost my big toes yesterday. Both of them. Do you know how hard it is to walk without big toes? Just makes catching something to eat that much harder. Looks like my right index finger is hanging on by a thread. But that doesn't mean I can't stop looking for something to eat.

I targeted my dinner back at the corner gas station a day or two ago. Old man with a penchant for classic country music and gun racks. Seemed to have a real fondness for Patsy Cline based on his ring tone. I hate country music.

Idiot had left his truck unlocked and I got his address from his registration. Don't these morons listen to the news? I snicker. If my plan works, *he'll* be on the eleven o'clock news. My dinner heads for the fried chicken place on the next block right after he fills up his shiny new truck. I peeked in the restaurant earlier; it was packed and this particular place was not known for its speedy service. I can hear Patsy Cline wail from his stereo as he turns into the drive-thru, and the zombie madness tickles the back of my brain. At least I'll hear him coming.

Scientists still don't know what causes the madness except that it's related to the Gene 69, more specifically the FAM69A which is a protein coding gene. They are always looking for subjects to experiment on, but it won't be me. I'll leave this planet in my own way – one piece at a time.

I drag, stumble, and shuffle my way towards his place, which for a normal is about a ten-minute walk, but takes me three times that long. Like I said, try walking without big toes. Not so easy. I take a shortcut across an abandoned baseball field reminding me of a battlefield in some foreign war I was in from a different life years ago.

The chain link fence twists toward the highway like a grotesque giant serpent crawling for an escape. Aluminum bleachers stand, the seats like a giant cracked ribcage dripping in blood, gore, and us. Some body parts still twitch ever so slightly, while some of us sprawl on the ground or lie in the batter's box with heads flung from their bodies like a foul ball. Left field shows some promise of a snack with scattered bodies lying around. I amble over to see if I might find something to eat. Nothing. Just more headless us, and we can't eat us. Normals discovered the best way to make sure we stayed dead was beheading. But still, you think they might have at least buried our remains. We were human once. Show some respect.

I find an aluminum bat with a good heft to use as a cane to help me along the way. It had some blood splatter and dents on it, but I didn't care. If I am lucky, it will have more splatter on it. One of my few remaining teeth falls out adding to the detritus on the ball field. Looks like the normals won this battle. I sigh and pick my way through the bodies and onto the sidewalk leading to Dinner's home.

Of course he has a hound dog. Dinner probably thinks of himself as a good hunter, but he's wrong. Not until he's on this side of the hunt. The dog yelps once when I hit it with the bat, and I gobble down its brains to help fight the madness, but its tiny brain is only a bite that won't last long. I need human brains to think clearly, to live a couple of more days to plan on how to survive. I hide the carcass in the bushes and wait, hidden in the shadows, at the back door for my human dinner.

Patsy Cline's voice warbles into the driveway and around to the back of the house; the song cuts off mid-verse. The smell of fried chicken mixed with exhaust fumes wafts into my sensitive nose, aggravating the madness. I shrink further into the shadows. Dinner fumbles with his door key; I notice his hands have that old man tremor. As I grip my aluminum bat for a swing, my right pinkie snaps off. Hell. It rolls like a shriveled sausage onto the back doorstep and squashes under his boot as he steps into the kitchen.

I ignore the gathering madness in my brain and swing. The bat cracks his head, fried chicken flies in slow motion scattering across the white ceramic kitchen floor. Dinner falls with a grunt. I crack his skull like hard-boiled egg. Blood pools beneath him. His leg twitches. A phone slides from his pants pocket, singing and vibrating in a mad frenzy of Patsy Cline's *I Fall to Pieces*. I pound it into silence.

Sitting on the leather sofa, I watch some black and white zombie movie on the big screen TV. I laugh. At least they got the walking part right.

I reach into the nearly empty fried chicken bucket. My tongue slobbers around my fingers, licking the last of the sticky brains from my knuckles and palm. The screen flickers as a zombie crashes through the window grabbing a screaming victim. I laugh so hard my left eye pops out and rolls under the TV. For the moment, I am full, content, and calm.

I guess I'll stay here until the madness snakes into my brain demanding another sacrifice. My left eye stares at the owner lying sprawled on the kitchen floor, twisted neck, a cavernous hole in the back of his skull. His plaid flannel shirt and blue jeans are sticky with blood. His hand is in a loose fist giving me a thumbs up and I laugh – a throaty, sticky laugh. Don't reckon he minds one bit.